Return
of the
Nutcracker
Prince

JASMINE C. CALDWELL

For my dad, who taught me to believe in magic

Chapter 1

Clara was having that dream again. Her godfather, Drosselmeyer, must have sent it. He was a magic old clock and toy maker that never seemed to get any older. A good friend of the Stahlbaums, Godfather Drosselmeyer was renowned for his intricate, unexplainable toys.

Mama and Papa never believed her as a child when she said Drosselmeyer sent her dreams. This particular one was far too similar to the dream she'd had that Christmas Eve when she was thirteen. It was the most frightening, and yet, her favorite dream.

In it, a Nutcracker fell from the grand tree in the ballroom. Her spoiled brat of a brother, Fritz, tried to fight her for it, using his new toy sword to smash its jaw when he wasn't allowed to play with it. Devastated, Clara pressed the piece back into his wooden face, kissed it, then Godfather Drosselmeyer wrapped his handkerchief around it like a bandage.

"Such a brave soldier," he said in that odd way of his. *"He shall never forget this."*

That all had actually happened that strange Christmas Eve. It was the rest that was a repeat of her dream.

Unable to sleep, Clara returned to the drawing room after the rest of the house went to bed, looking for her Nutcracker soldier. But huge, human-sized mice crept into the ballroom, seeking the crumbs left after the party. When she squealed in terror, they attacked.

Just when she was surrounded, the Nutcracker burst into life, coming to her aid with his large wooden head and his sword slashing. Fritz's toy soldiers marched on the invaders at the Nutcracker's command, but the Mouse King appeared from beneath the floor and turned the tide of the battle against her and her protector.

"Prince, I have you now!" She shuddered in her sleep at the giant, seven-headed rodent's hiss. Unwilling to merely sit by and watch as he towered over them, Clara threw her only weapon, her slipper, at his center head.

Miraculously, the slipper not only hit its mark, it reduced the monster to the size of a normal one-headed mouse. Smaller than even his subjects, the Mouse King fled. The Nutcracker gave chase, and she followed him through a strange portal. On the other side, his wooden head had disappeared, and standing before her was a boy.

This was her favorite part of the dream. The prince appeared to be close to her age, with the build of a young soldier. He had dark brown hair and bewitching blue eyes. She could tell it was him by his red and gold uniform. By a frozen lake surrounded by snow, he fell to one knee and took her hand.

"My Lady, I owe you my life. I am Klaus; what is your name?"

"Clara."

He took her on a tour of this dream kingdom, ending in a celebration of Klaus's return and the Mouse King's defeat. This is where the dream got fuzzy, except for the very end.

"Look, we're under the mistletoe."

Her cheeks burned hot as she turned her face upwards, spying a sprig of that infamous plant.

"May I?"

It was a dream anyway, right? With wide eyes and a dry mouth, she could only nod. Hesitantly, Klaus leaned in and pressed his lips to hers. A strange tingle buzzed her mouth, and she closed her eyes. This didn't feel like a dream. This felt... real.

Then, just like the first time she had this dream, she woke up in her own bed, lips aflame and heart racing.

As the red sun set in the violet sky, Klaus ran through the orchard to his uncle's workshop. He'd told his parents he was retiring early, only to slip from the palace with them none the wiser. Light still shone in the window of the small wooden building tucked at the edge of the Sugar Plum Palace grounds. Thank the Goddess! He hadn't missed his window. Bursting through the cinnamon wood door, Klaus entreated the old man. "Uncle Ludwig, you *must* take me with you tonight!"

Still bending over his bag, Klaus's uncle raised his head, his eye patch hiding his one purple eye. Barren shelves surrounded them, the tables strewn with tools and scraps from last-minute revisions. All the toys were in the gray fabric sack in front of the white-haired man standing before him.

"Good evening, nephew." Ludwig Drosselmeyer chuckled. "Have you discussed this with your parents?"

"There's no time! The mice are nearly at our door, and we need help. They wouldn't understand, anyway."

Uncle Ludwig rubbed his chin in thought. "Are you sure you don't just want to see *her* again?"

Klaus sighed in exasperation. Ten years before, he'd snuck into Uncle Ludwig's sack of toys for the children of the Stahlbaum Christmas party. Upon finding him, he'd begged his uncle to hide his wooden Nutcracker form in the tree, so he could see what it was all about. Then Clara appeared.

Fierce, brave Clara, with her soft brown eyes, and softer lips. When the mice attacked, it had been *her* who had defeated the Mouse King, not he. But his parents had never believed him. He'd brought her to his realm and shown her around, then had his first kiss under the holy mistletoe in the Land of Sweets and Toys. According to the legend in his world, that meant Clara was his true love, that fate chose them for each other. But they could only be together if she came to this realm again. He was stuck in his wooden doll form when he traveled to her world.

He'd been a boy then. But the feelings he had for her, the dreams of seeing her again, were still there. Father and Mother were starting to make noises about finding him a princess, ensuring stability for the Sugar Plum kingdom.

Klaus had yet to tell them who he wanted.

"Which answer results in you taking me with you?"

Uncle Ludwig sighed and opened his pack. "Take care not to get caught by the mice this time. Your father will skin me alive if it happens again."

"Thank you, Uncle!"

He stepped into the fabric. Uncle Ludwig opened the portal to the Realm of Waking. Its blue light growing rapidly until the other world came into view. Beyond the portal stood the stately bricks of Stahlbaum manor. Warmth glowed from every window and door, welcoming the guests for the annual Christmas Eve festivities. That was the last thing he saw as the uncomfortable stiffness of his Nutcracker form overtook him. He shrank into the sack as Uncle Ludwig hefted it onto his shoulder. Soon, he would see his Clara again.

After all this time, would she remember him?

Footsteps marched down the hallway. Clara recognized her mother's gait over the steam of the laundry room. "Heidi, could you press these linens and take them down to the drawing room? They're for the desserts table."

"Of course, Miss Clara." The young maid's cap bobbled as she curtsied, cradling the delicate damask.

"Thank you," Clara responded, flustered. The way the servants deferred to her now that she was an adult always made her uncomfortable.

Heidi and she were both twenty-three, yet merely by the circumstances of their birth, they had fallen into drastically different roles in society. Clara's maid had gone to the local schoolhouse until she reached working age. Her reading and writing were elementary, and she could add or subtract enough to handle her meager pay. Meanwhile, Clara and Fritz had been tutored by a private governess, and her father's library was always open to her to expand her mind. While many girls of her station enjoyed their embroidery lessons, Clara had always escaped as quickly as possible into a book. Sticking her fingers with needles was not her idea of a pleasant pastime.

She'd never felt right treating Heidi, or any other servant, as a lesser person. They did not choose their life any more than she herself had. But Margareta Stahlbaum did not agree with her approach.

Clara took a deep breath and braced herself for her mother's harsh tongue. She must have overheard her thanking Heidi and stormed into the room, her fierce green eyes shooting sparks. Heidi scurried out and away from the mistress of the house.

"Clara, what do I always tell you?"

Her gaze fell to the floor, unable to meet her mother's smoldering ire. "The servants are not your friends."

"The servants are not your friends," Margareta repeated. "They are here to do a job. And it is your right and your duty to tell them what to do. Your father pays them and you owe them nothing more."

Clara's face burned in shame. Not at what she had done, but because she wasn't the least bit sorry. It was an old argument, one her mother had lectured her on for years. She'd learned long ago it was easier to stay silent when she inevitably displeased her mother.

"Your next embroidery shall be 'A mouse cannot run a house.' And why are you concerning yourself with the linens? The head housekeeper knows what is required. She doesn't need you."

She remained silent. Clara knew better than to tell her mother she enjoyed feeling useful. Mrs. Schafer had asked to borrow Heidi because one of the other maids had come down with a cold. She had wanted to help like she used to. Before the servants changed how they treated her.

Her heart ached for her lost childhood.

"Now, the party will start in less than an hour and you're still wearing your day dress. Go get ready. And have your maid pull your stays tighter; all those sweets you've been eating have done you no favors." With that last dig at her plump figure, the slim, elegant Margareta swept back out into the hallway.

Clara waited until her mother was gone and then stole out the servant's staircase to avoid anyone else seeing her. Fritz would have a field day if he knew Mama had scolded her. That golden boy could do no wrong in their mother's eyes and it grated on her. His favorite hobbies were horseback riding and bullying his elder sister.

Even the thought of finally wearing her beautiful green silk Christmas gown, brand new this year, couldn't brighten her spirits. She'd never been the daughter Margareta wanted; too sympathetic, too emotional. And far too invested in her books.

As a child, when she'd tried to tell her parents about the fantastic dreams she had at night, her mother would say, *Stop telling tales.*

It had been years since she dreamed regularly. Which was why the dream from the night before had been so odd.

But Fritz waited upstairs in the hall, buttoning his brown silk waistcoat. "Where have you been?"

"Around." She didn't need to answer to her little brother.

While he was much more pleasant nowadays, since they were adults, Fritz still lived to pester her. He just didn't break her things anymore. Papa made him work in the stable last time, for an entire week two years ago, to pay him back for the last perfume bottle he'd shattered.

It had been her favorite, too.

"You'll never get a husband if you insist on hiding in the library."

The joke was on him; she didn't want one.

Silence was best deployed when dealing with Fritz. Clara had learned that a long time ago. She slammed her door in his face and sighed.

Heidi knocked gently on her door shortly thereafter. "Miss Clara, your mother sent me to help you dress."

"Come in."

Her maid and best friend slipped inside and shut the door, head bowed. And then she knew her mother had said something.

"Heidi, I'm so sorry. What did Mama say to you?"

Raising her chin, Heidi appeared to brush off Margareta's words once more. "It was nothing, Miss. Shall I help you undress?"

"Of course." Resigned, she turned her back to her maid so she could begin unhooking the cotton bodice.

"You mustn't use the servant's stairs again, Miss Clara. Your mother doesn't like it."

"I simply couldn't bear to see anyone after talking with her."

"But you're already receiving guests. The Galen family, including young Berengar, is here to see your father."

"Then I am especially pleased I did not use the main staircase." She saw Heidi's smirk in the mirror. She knew Clara had no love for her brother's friend. Berengar had often made jokes at her expense, much to Fritz's delight. He was as much of a ruffian as Fritz.

It made no difference to her if they had arrived early.

Once she'd removed the day dress, Heidi produced two additional petticoats to layer under the evening gown.

"Heidi," Clara sighed. "Mother asked that you tighten my stays before tonight."

"But you'll barely be able to breathe!"

"Please, Heidi. I would rather not risk any more of her wrath tonight. It's Christmas Eve, after all."

"Very well, Miss." Laying the petticoats on the bed, Heidi got to work loosening the four petticoats she already wore, then did as she'd asked. Clara gasped.

"Are you alright? It's too much..."

"No, I'm fine. Leave it, Heidi." If she fainted, her mother would simply have to excuse her from the festivities. She tried to shake off her foul mood. After all, her friends would be there. It'd been ages since she'd seen Adelia and Francesca.

After her undergarments were back in place, Heidi slipped the additional petticoats over her head, followed by her gown. The off-the-shoulder masterpiece had a pointed bodice, which elongated her plump torso and gave the illusion of a slimmer figure. A white lace bertha hung from the *en coer* neckline, enhancing her decolletage.

"Miss Clara, you look radiant," Heidi gasped as she hooked the bodice together in the back.

"It's a beautiful dress." But Heidi was right. The green silk highlighted her golden hair and brought out her brown eyes. She looked elegant, like a voluptuous version of her mother.

Margareta would have no reason to complain again tonight.

"You're a Christmas angel. And that has nothing to do with the gown."

She turned to Heidi, who was starting to speak like herself again. She smiled.

"Thank you, Heidi."

Her secret friend grinned back at her. "Let's get your hair curled."

Chapter 2

Clara still had some time before the party began. In her new silk gown, with her hair curled prettily around the pearl circlet her papa had gifted her for Christmas ten years ago, she looked like a princess.

And felt like it too, trapped in a tower with no way out.

Well, she did have one, albeit a temporary way. Reading had always been her escape. Anxious to fill her time before the party, Clara crept into her father's library. Dark wood shelves lined the walls, laden with leather-bound volumes. Most of them were Papa's ledgers, but he had plenty of fiction as well. She pulled down an old favorite, caressing the worn cover. There was time for a quick chapter before the party.

No sooner had she settled into a chair than the door opened. "Ah, there you are." Papa let Mama into the library and shut the door behind them. Clara laid the unopened book on her lap.

"Clara. Your father has fantastic news."

"Yes, Papa?"

Her father clapped his hands and puffed out his chest. "My dear, you have a suitor."

"A suitor." Who could it be? Her brows furrowed in confusion.

"Yes, the von Galens came to me today to discuss a marriage between you and their son."

But their only son was... "Berengar?"

"The very same."

No. No, no, no *no!* She tried to wipe her clammy hands on the book in her lap. "But Berengar despises me." She hated how her voice trembled.

Finally, Mama spoke. "It's time for both of you to grow up past this silly childish nonsense. The von Galens are a fine family. By the wedding next year, you will be ready to be a proper wife." Margareta's glare showed that her lessons in embroidery and commanding servants would soon become more intense.

Clara's breaths became short, and she inwardly cursed that she had insisted Heidi tighten her corset. This urge to please her parents would be the death of her.

Papa drew closer and kneeled down so he could look her in the eye. "I know it's a lot to take in. But don't worry about it right now." Clara could hardly register the remorse on his face; she was so shocked at this betrayal.

He must have expected a more positive reaction, but she didn't care about how much money this other family had. She cared about how their son had treated her. And somehow her own dear Papa had promised her hand to that brute.

"We won't be announcing it right away. Baron von Galen didn't want to overshadow the Christmas Eve celebrations, so we're going to announce it at the New Year's Eve party. That will give you time to get used to the idea."

She only had one week to come to terms with the worst announcement in her life. And now she had to go to the Christmas Eve party and pretend nothing was wrong. Clara tried to swallow the lump in her throat. Of her twenty-three Christmases, this was the worst.

"We need to greet the guests, Friedrich." Mama reminded him.

"Yes, the guests. I'm coming, my love."

Papa rose and linked Mama's arm through his and turned to leave.

"May I..." When she spoke, they turned their heads. "May I speak with Mama for a moment, please?"

Margareta patted her husband's arm and turned back to Clara, a gentle smile on her face. Once the door had shut behind Papa, she asked, "Are you frightened, my daughter?"

"I — yes!" How did Mama know?

"The first time is painful. I won't lie to you. But after that, it's much better."

Oh heavens. That's not at all what she had meant!

Her face heated as she stammered. "No, Mama. That's not it." She shook her head. "I just, I always wanted what you and Papa have. I want a husband who loves me." Not a bully.

Despite how her heart hurt, in her head, Clara knew her parents loved her in their own ways. Papa gave her far more leniency than her peers' fathers, having never found an educated woman intimidating. Mama meant well with her lectures, but neither fully understood what Clara desired, nor, she feared, did they care.

Margareta held her arms out and Clara accepted one of her rare hugs. "My dear child, your papa did not love me when we married. Nor did I love him. The love happened gradually. It will come in time."

Her heart sank as her mother released her and nodded at her in encouragement. "Now it's time for the party. Put the book away and come on down."

She took the time to pat at her eyes with her handkerchief before placing the novel back on the shelf. Clara had realized a long time ago that life would force her to shelve her books one day. Many women her age had long been married and were already mothers. Still, the thought of becoming Mrs. Berengar von Galen felt as though someone were cutting out her heart with a rusted spoon.

She didn't want to be a peacock in a gilded cage. But what choice did she have?

Gathering her wits, Clara made her way down the hall to the drawing room where her parents stood welcoming their guests. There would be time to cry after the party when she lay in her bed. Happy Christmas, indeed.

She stood next to her mother and played the dutiful daughter. Thankfully, the von Galens were already enjoying the festivities. Berengar was surely notifying his best friend Fritz that they were to be brothers-in-law.

She prayed Fritz wouldn't ruin the party by announcing her fate early.

"Happy Christmas, Stahlbaum family!" Clara's childhood friend burst with delight as she and her family entered the house.

"Adelia!" The two friends had not seen each other since Adelia had married Franz. "Who is this?" She gestured at the bundle of blankets her dear friend carried.

"This is my son, Josef."

She peered at the tiny pink face as his mother pulled back the blanket protecting him from the cold. "He's beautiful, Adelia."

Francesca and her husband, Johann, appeared as well, and the trio of women shared a joyful reunion.

"You look amazing, Clara. Did you get my last letter?"

"I did, but I hadn't the chance to write back yet. Congratulations." Francesca had confided in her that after years of trying, she was to be blessed with a baby in the summer.

This year's party couldn't be terrible with her old friends by her side.

The last guest to arrive always used to put a huge smile on her face. He wore his signature aubergine top hat, the same old gray overcoat, and his black eye patch over his left eye.

"Friedrich! Margareta! A happy Christmas to you both!" Godfather Drosselmeyer shuffled in, laden with his bag of presents for the children.

"Happy Christmas to you as well, Godfather Drosselmeyer." Papa smiled brilliantly, and Mama curtsied as their honored guest kissed the back of her hand. Servants whisked away his hat and coat. Then her godfather stood before her and bowed.

"It's always good to see you, Godpapa."

"My dear Clara, you look lovely tonight. You do so take after your mother."

Clara curtsied, but her attempt at a smile didn't fool him.

He pulled her aside and looked around with glittering, mischievous eyes. "I have just the thing to cheer you up, child." Reaching into his bag, the white-haired man produced a familiar wooden soldier. Dark hair, painted blue eyes, a golden crown on his head, and a bright red uniform.

"My Nutcracker! Oh, Godfather..." Her face fell as Mama's words came back to her. But she couldn't be rude in the face of the one gift she'd wanted for the last ten years. "I love him. Thank you ever so much."

"What's troubling you?"

"I'm afraid I'm too old for Christmas presents such as this." Tears stung the back of her eyes as she pushed the emotions down and whispered the awful truth. "I'm grown up now. And Papa has decided I shall marry Berengar next year." Try as she might, she couldn't keep the disdain out of her voice as she spoke his name.

The Nutcracker's jaw dropped as she lifted him up to see him one last time.

"You're never too old for this sort of present," Godfather Drosselmeyer assured her, pushing the Nutcracker back into her arms. "You're a dreamer, Clara."

She sighed and repeated the mantra Mama had drilled into her head since childhood. "Dreams don't mean anything."

"No, child. Dreams mean *everything*." The strange man gave her his quirky grin. "And some of them are true."

What did he mean, they were true?

"Listen to me, child." Drosselmeyer motioned to her to get closer, then spoke in her ear. "Take him to the clock at the stroke of twelve. You don't want the mice to catch him again."

She furrowed her brows at his words, but her eyes widened. Drosselmeyer *did* send her dreams. She knew it!

Then Drosselmeyer did the strangest thing. He spoke to the *Nutcracker*.

"Klaus, I will send two horses to the other side of the portal in the Enchanted Forest. You will have one hour. The mice will be sufficiently distracted, but I can't be sure their Seers didn't find you again. Stay vigilant." Then Drosselmeyer winked at her and turned away.

Clara stood there, flabbergasted. Perhaps her godfather was as crazy as everyone said!

Were Klaus in his true form, he'd be sweating. His Clara was engaged to another? He cursed his current state, but there was nothing he could do except lie in her arms while his uncle passed out toys from his magical sack of gifts. She kept him pressed to her breast, as if worried that someone would take him from her.

When the dancing began, a dark-haired woman dressed in a pale blue gown approached them.

"Daughter, there you are. The grand promenade is about to begin. Berengar is waiting for you."

"Mama..."

"You need to dance with your intended, my dear. Put the Nutcracker down. No one will bother him on the table there."

As much as he wanted to stay right where he was, Klaus got his first proper look at Clara when she set him down behind her. She'd grown into a young woman with ripe curves that stole his breath. Her golden hair and chocolate brown eyes remained the same. And she looked at him so sadly... Goddess, how he longed to take her in his arms!

Then she took a deep breath and strode to her place on the dance floor with her head held high. Pride swelled within him; she was just as fierce as he remembered.

By the end of the song, Klaus was ready to use this Berengar as a dummy for his next training session with his saber. He held Clara so close she stiffened and kept putting distance between them. Her smile was nowhere to be seen, and as they passed him, he caught snippets of what her fiancé said to her.

"Women have no business reading."

"Fat cows are good for carrying babies."

"Women should be seen and not heard," was his response when she tried to stand up for herself.

Klaus's wooden skin crawled at hearing those words and watching Clara get more and more uncomfortable. When the swine said, "I can't wait to breed you," she dropped his hand like a hot poker. Thankfully, the song was over. She spun on her heel and sped away into a circle of women her age. They embraced as old friends, and Berengar, ignored, stalked away.

This was unacceptable! Clara's parents clearly did not know how terrible this man was that they had promised their daughter to. Not to mention the Goddess had chosen her to be with *him*. The mistletoe had spoken.

Uncle Ludwig, I beg you, take the next dance with Clara. Please don't let her dance with that sorry excuse for a man again. In his Nutcracker form, Klaus had one method of communication, and it only worked with others from his realm. How Ludwig remained flesh in this realm was beyond Klaus's comprehension, but his uncle *was* a rare male Dreamer with magic.

It would be my pleasure. He responded and started moving across the room towards her.

Breathing a sigh of relief, Klaus looked at the grandfather clock with the owl atop it.

He had three more hours left of this torture. Then he could explain everything, and ask her to return to the Land of Sweets with him once more. Klaus just knew she could save his kingdom, and in return, he could protect her from this Berengar.

Adelia and Francesca comforted Clara after the disaster that was her dance with Berengar von Galen.

"Why on earth would you dance with him?" Adelia asked her.

"Mother asked it of me." She kept her back to the room, not ready to explain why.

"Well, it's over now." Francesca patted her shoulder. "Hopefully, your next dance partner will be more pleasant."

But Clara didn't want to dance anymore. She swallowed a groan when someone tapped her shoulder. Turning, she beheld Godfather Drosselmeyer in a deep bow with his hand extended.

"May I have this dance?" he asked as the musicians began a cotillion.

With a genuine, relieved smile, she placed her hand in his. "Of course, Godfather."

The goofy Drosselmeyer knew how to make Clara laugh. He danced just slightly out of sync with the harpsichord, spinning too far, then landing with a mischievous grin that revealed he knew exactly what he was doing. Her godfather saved the Christmas Eve party for her by deflecting Berengar and making comments about his behavior close enough for the von Galens to overhear. Too bad her Papa was so set on her marrying the ratbag.

The hour grew late, and the guests departed. Adelia and Francesca left with their husbands, nannies, and children in tow. The von Galens' farewell was stiff, with Berengar on his best behavior.

Exhausted, she retired to her bedroom, where Heidi waited to help her out of her gown.

"How was the party, Miss Clara?" Heidi asked as deft fingers opened the hooks at the back of the bodice and lifted the emerald silk over her head.

"It was perfectly lovely. Except for the news Mama and Papa gave me beforehand." Dread weighted her limbs, and she sank onto her bed after her stays and petticoats came off. Heidi pulled her pearl circlet from her head and placed it in its velvet-lined box. Then she unpinned Clara's hair so she could brush it for bed.

"What news?"

"I'm to be married next year," she groaned.

Heidi gasped and jumped off the bed. "But that's wonderful! Congratulations. Who's the lucky groom?"

"Berengar von Galen."

Her maid's expression fell as she sat back down. "You have my deepest condolences, Miss." She resumed taking out the pins from her hair, handing over her brush as she finished. As Clara brushed it out, she remembered her gift.

"Oh no! I left my Nutcracker in the drawing room!"

"Shall I fetch it for you?"

"I'd like to get him myself. Quick, hand me my nightclothes." Fritz had broken her beloved Nutcracker out of jealousy once before, and she couldn't risk him finding it before she did. He might not break her things anymore, but she didn't trust him not to steal it, just to upset her.

Wrapped in her slippers and night robe, she padded down through the house, with only her melancholy thoughts for company. How could Papa *do* this to her? Mama hadn't ever really liked her. She told too many stories and hid in the library instead of socializing. But she thought she had a special connection with Papa. That he appreciated her intellect. Yet he wanted to waste it with the von Galen's lout of a son. Didn't he love her at all?

Slipping into the drawing room, she spied the little wooden man on the table just as the grandfather clock chimed the hour.

Midnight.

By the second bong, she had crossed the floor. The Nutcracker shook, moving forward bit by bit. On the third chime, he fell off the table without Clara or anything touching him. It was as if... no, that was impossible. He couldn't throw *himself* off the table, could he?

She thought for sure he'd break. Instead, a bright light shone from the Nutcracker, and he hovered off the floor.

"What in heaven's name...?"

Growing in size while the clock chimed on, her wooden Nutcracker transformed into a man!

Chapter 3

K laus's feet settled onto the floor, his eyes taking a moment to adjust to the dim light. Clara stood in front of him in a white robe, holding a single candle. Now that he was in his full form again, she was the perfect height. He could hold her in his arms and lay her head on his shoulder. They'd fit perfectly together. Her hair flowing down her back glowed like a halo. For a moment, he let his starving eyes feast on her once more.

"Clara…"

She startled and jumped backward. "How do you know my name?"

"It's me. Klaus." At her confused expression, he could have smacked himself. Of course, she didn't recognize him. It'd been far too long, and they weren't children anymore.

"Do you remember Christmas Eve ten years ago?" She nodded warily. "I had snuck into my uncle's bag that year without his knowledge. When he found me, he placed me in the tree. But I fell out, and you caught me."

Her brow furrowed, but she nodded. "That was how I found the Nutcracker, and Godfather Drosselmeyer gave him to me. But..." She squinted her eyes at him. "Godfather is your uncle?"

"Yes. My Uncle Ludwig." He took a deep breath and continued, "That night, the mice attacked and nearly overwhelmed me."

Clara blinked her brown eyes and shook her head. "No..." she seemed to talk to herself. "The mice were part of the dream."

"No, they were *real*." He chanced taking a step closer. "And so was the way you defeated their king."

A shudder ran through her, no doubt remembering her first glimpse of the grotesque demon. "I don't understand."

"You were the last one to defeat him, and not only has he returned to full power, he's stronger than ever." In desperation, Klaus took her free hand in both of his. "Do you remember my country, the Land of Sweets and Toys? It's the only free land left in my realm." His heart beat out a march in his chest. "You went with me to visit that night." She nodded, staring at him like *he* was the one with seven heads. "We kissed under the mistletoe."

With a sharp intake of her breath, Clara snatched her hand back. "Impossible."

"It's the truth!"

Her chest rose and plunged with her breath. "I'm dreaming."

"I may be a Dreamer, but I am no dream."

"How do I know you're telling the truth?" She wasn't taking her eyes off his face.

Turning his head, he let the light hit the scar on his jaw. "When I was in Nutcracker form ten years ago, your brother attacked me with his toy sword and broke part of my chin. It healed, but you can see the mark it left." Clara gasped and tentatively raised her hand, then pulled it away. "Go on. Feel for yourself."

Her gentle fingers traced the line on his jaw, and Klaus turned his head into her touch. But he was running out of time. The longer it took to convince her, the closer the mice could be to finding him. How could he express this need? When she drew her hand back once more, he did the only thing he could think of — Klaus fell to his knees, clutching it and kissing her knuckles. "Clara, as Prince of Süssland, I beg you to help us defeat the Mouse King once and for all."

Elation filled him as she slowly nodded.

"Yes. Yes, I will help you. If I can..."

He leaped to his feet and cupped her face with both hands. Her doe eyes were wide, the sweet curve of her lips tempting him. "I can hardly believe this; I have dreamed of you for so long..." But as he bent his head, she slipped away.

"Klaus... I am to marry Berengar. Our parents will announce our engagement in one week's time. I must return by then. That's... all I can give you." She looked away, her free arm wrapped around her middle. Did she actually want the bastard?

The tearing sound he heard was surely his heart ripping in two. "As you wish."

An awkward silence descended, and Klaus could have heard a pin drop.

Or... paws scrabbling on marble floors.

Their heads shot up as they realized the enemy had discovered them. Klaus grabbed her hand as squeaking erupted in the walls, the mouse language impossible to interpret. Clara blew her candle out and dropped the candlestick on the marble floor as they bolted to the grandfather clock. The door opened and Klaus jumped through, pulling her behind him.

Blue lights surrounded them as they fell down the portal Uncle Ludwig had left behind. Gingersnaps! It had opened up several feet in the air! Klaus turned to face her, wrapping his arms around her.

"Klaus!" She tried to push away.

"Trust me!" Seconds later, his back slammed into the ground. Klaus shook his head. When his vision cleared, they lay among the ancient pine trees of the Enchanted Forest. A neutral zone, with no one but the stag and fox to rule. Clara scrambled to get off him, then he rose himself.

"I just didn't want you to get hurt." He raised his hands. "I apologize."

"Thank you." Her eyes were full of wonder as she took in their surroundings. "Where are we?"

"The Enchanted Forest. Uncle Ludwig said he'd send horses for us." He took a deep breath of the winter night air. Only slivers of moonlight broke through the trees here. A whinny ahead of them drew his attention.

"Pepper!" Tied to a tree further into the forest was Klaus's beloved horse Peppermint, a black stallion. Next to him was Tinsel, a familiar mare. She was a horse in the royal stables, usually used for training. She'd be the perfect horse for Clara to ride.

Klaus plodded through the snow and turned back to see her shivering as she followed. "Wh-why do you call it the Enchanted F-forest?"

"Because of its magic. Here, let me show you." He called out to the trees. "We need a warm coat for Clara."

"P-please."

"Please," he added. Funny, he'd never thought about manners when addressing the forest. But then he'd grown up here. Asking the Enchanted Forest for something you needed was commonplace. The trees would provide if they could.

The branches above them rustled, and down dropped a fine woolen cloak in midnight blue. Clara's mouth dropped open. "Th-thank you!" Then she struggled to wrap it around herself with her shaking hands until Klaus stepped in. He tied it fast under her chin and flipped the hood up over her golden hair. She was the absolute vision of a winter beauty.

And he *had* to remember she was betrothed to another.

Stepping back, he led her to the horses, who pranced back and forth on their hooves, probably eager to get going. "Here, this fine girl is Tinsel. Let's get you mounted —"

Just then, a bullet shot from the darkness of the forest and landed on Tinsel's rump. With a frightened neigh, the brown horse reared and bolted.

"No!"

"Hurry, get on Peppermint. We're out of time."

Klaus lifted Clara into Peppermint's saddle, her legs dangling over the side, then drew his sword. She clutched the reins with white-knuckled hands. In the shadows of the forest, a small troop of four human-sized mice in blue coats and tall black hats rammed bullets down their rifles. Their leader, dressed in puffy pants and a vest, advanced on Klaus with his cutlass drawn.

Back in the drawing room, she decided she must have fallen asleep instead of going after her Nutcracker. Now, she was amidst the strangest dream of all. Godfather Drosselmeyer must have planted the seed of it in her mind at that party. It all felt so real; the bite of the snow through her slippers, the wind rustling the branches of the trees. The warmth of Klaus's cheek against her hand.

From her vantage point atop Peppermint, she realized the riflemen were merely back-up. The mouse wielding the cutlass was doing all the work. Peppermint's rear end danced away from the fight as swords clashed. She watched in helpless fear as the strange blade nearly overwhelmed Klaus, clutching the reins and her cloak to her chest. This might be a dream, but she still cared about him! If he died, would she wake?

His saber slipped over the cutlass's curved blade and right into the captain's shoulder. The mouse released an indignant squeak. Then Klaus was on the attack, pushing the captain back into the forest. His sword sang and the riflemen chattered, unsure where to aim their guns.

But the mouse captain had not finished yet. With a mighty kick from his huge back foot, Klaus flew into the clearing and landed on his back with a grunt. As he rose, the soldiers lowered their rifles to aim right at Klaus.

Her Nutcracker Prince. Her savior.

A burning need filled Clara's chest to bursting. She couldn't hold back her scream.

"*Stop*!"

Bright light eclipsed the clearing. The riflemen fired, but the bullets stopped in midair. A shielding wall of white light had formed around her, Klaus, and Peppermint.

"Klaus!"

Mounting Peppermint with a leap, he took up the reins with one hand, the other holding onto her. "Yah!" The big black stallion sprang into a gallop, his hooves kicking up snow and mud as they made their getaway.

In awe, she dared to look back. The wall of light shattered after they were gone from the clearing, and the mice gave chase. But Peppermint had greater speed, and soon they were a mere speck in the distance.

Their mount wove and dove through the trees. "What about Tinsel?"

"Tinsel will find her way home. She knows the way."

"But she's injured!"

Even her untrained eye could see the spots of blood marking the other horse's path in the snow.

"What if she tires herself out and doesn't make it?" Clara shivered and fought back tears. She would never forgive herself; it was her fault that they hadn't gotten away in time.

Klaus pulled back on the reins, checking behind him while Pepper slowed to a trot. "Alright. We'll try to find her and lead her home with us. She probably won't let a rider on with that injury."

Pepper's hooves turned to the right, following the tracks left in the snow. They passed broken branches and clods of ice and mud churned up by a frightened mare.

"Should we call her?"

"I'm afraid that will give away our location. The mice may have gone back to their king to report, but that doesn't mean he doesn't have spies out here." Klaus's keen blue eyes trained on the ground ahead. "Keep an eye on the sun. We must get back before dawn."

"Why?"

"Because I'd rather my parents didn't find out I've been gone all night."

His parents. The rulers of this strange land who needed help to defeat the Mouse King.

For a moment, she wondered if this was truly a dream, or if she'd gone completely mad. But she'd help them, no matter if this was real or not. If she woke up one morning back in her bed, so be it.

She took advantage of his proximity to inspect her rescuer in the moonlight and to reconcile his face with the boy she'd dreamed of previously. There was the pale thin scar from when her horrid little brother had damaged her Nutcracker. His uniform hadn't changed, transforming into a handsome red jacket and pants with gold buttons and epaulets. It was smudged and worn with the dirt of battle, but hopefully his people could repair it. His dark brown hair was cut short in a military style, and unlike most men of her country, he grew no hair on his face. Not even a side beard.

Clara wouldn't complain. Why should he cover that handsome cheek with prickly hair? The enchanting blue eyes had stayed the same. That's how she knew this was her Klaus.

Her Klaus? Where had that come from? And while she had been protective of her Nutcracker at the party, she could not lay claim to a flesh and blood man, even in her dreams. Especially when she was betrothed to Berengar.

She choked back the bile that hit the back of her throat. It would be best not to think of him.

The hunt for Tinsel came to a halt at the entrance to a thicket. Here, the moonlight could not pierce the eerily silent shadows.

"I can't go any further," Klaus whispered. "That leads to Blumenland, and it's under the Mouse King's control. It would lead us straight to him."

"Is she in there?"

"I don't know. I can't be sure. She may have gone home already, and we lost the trail."

Her heart sank. "I'm so sorry."

Klaus tugged on the reins, and Pepper backed up so they could turn. "It's getting late, and we need to get to Süssland. Once we're there, we'll be safe."

She braced herself for the lecture. If this were her brother, he'd never forgive her for causing him to lose one of his horses. Mama would have surely berated her as well.

But nothing came.

"Aren't you angry?" Why did she ask that? Perhaps he was so angry he couldn't speak, and she'd just invited him to yell.

"Of course I'm angry. The Mouse King has been destroying the entire realm."

"I, uh… that's not what I meant."

Klaus looked down at her incredulously as he pressed Peppermint back into a gallop once they reached a field.

"Am I angry at you? Gingersnaps, no! It's not your fault. This is the reality of war. We're blessed to have gotten out of there unharmed."

Out of the corner of her eye, a wall made of a strange-looking brown stone came into view. "The mice outnumbered us severely, and if anything happened to you, I'd never forgive myself." He paused, and his gaze caressed her face in a way that made her shiver with something other than cold. "You're far more important than a horse."

Clara blinked at him. She'd never heard that before. In her world, women weren't much better off than horses. At least in her opinion.

Now she *knew* she was dreaming.

"We're here," Klaus said, breaking her out of her thoughts. In front of them, a large gate of thick red and white peppermint sticks rose into the sky, permitting them to pass. "The guards saw me coming. Let's ask about Tinsel."

She looked up in amazement as Klaus directed Peppermint under the portcullis. It immediately dropped behind them. He walked his steed over to a trough standing off to the side of the gate, then dismounted and tied Pepper to a post.

Reaching for her, Klaus's smile dazzled her in the early morning light. "Welcome back to the Land of Sweets and Toys."

Chapter 4

"Prince Klaus!" The guard on duty climbed down a striped candy ladder from the ramparts and ran up to Klaus while his saddle partner gazed around, speechless.

"My thanks for the swift entry; we were running from the Mouse Army."

The young soldier saluted him. "We were not aware you had left the Land of Sweets."

"You weren't supposed to." Klaus cursed his lack of foresight. Of course, now word would get back to his parents that he had been away. "The mice attacked, and we lost sight of our injured mare. Did she come by here?"

"A brown horse with Süssland crimson and gold ran through about an hour ago, like the devil was on her tail."

That drew Clara's attention. "What about her injury?"

The guard shook his head. "We couldn't catch her, Miss."

"Listen, Private, er…"

The young man's spine straightened, and he saluted once more. "Private Gebäck, Your Highness."

"Private Gebäck, I would appreciate it if you and your contingent could keep my entrance here from reaching the palace. I should like to explain my actions to the Sugar Plum Fairy myself. We are making our way there now."

"I will tell the others, My Prince."

"You have my thanks." Peppermint was slurping from the trough, which someone had just refreshed. He patted the long equine neck and felt more than heard him snort.

"Can you get us home, old friend?"

Pepper raised his head and snorted once more, then pushed his nose into Klaus's hand. He chuckled. "Very well, you shall have some pets first."

As a boy, when he wasn't dodging his lessons or fencing with his tutor, Klaus could often be found in the stables. He loved the freeing feeling of riding, and the horses never cared about his rank. They'd happily melt the stresses of the palace away in exchange for the treats in his pocket.

Clara approached them. "May I pet him as well?"

"I'm sure he'd love nothing more." The two of them rubbed his horse affectionately, and Klaus stuffed down his jealousy that Pepper got to feel her touch.

"He's a beautiful animal. And he's so brave, too."

"Careful, or you'll give him a big head," Klaus teased. Pepper grunted and turned his head around on his neck to bump her with it.

"I see how it is. You like her better, do you?" Klaus laughed, and Clara's cheeks turned pink. She kept rubbing his horse down, and he wanted to make her smile like that as much as possible.

Animals could sense a person's heart, and Peppermint's approval of her made Klaus ache for more than a week with her. But part of her appeal was her dedication to her family, as misguided as they may be.

"Ready to go home, boy?" He turned away to hide his frown and watched the horse's reaction. Satisfied that he'd had enough water and rest, Klaus reached out a hand. "May I help you up?"

"That's alright, I can mount with the stirrups." Clara lifted herself up with the saddle, but her nightgown didn't give her enough room to get her leg over Peppermint's back. Klaus caught her just as she lost her grip.

"It would be my pleasure," he assured her.

"But Klaus, I'm too — oh." He'd hoisted her right into the saddle, seated to the side as she had been before.

"I beg your pardon. You were saying?"

Her face turned bright red. "I was only worried you would hurt yourself."

"I'm fine." Klaus put his weight on the stirrup and lifted himself into the saddle behind her. It was a tight fit, but he didn't care. He gathered the reins and turned Peppermint onto the main road.

"You're leaving him at a walk?"

"I don't want to tire him out. And we're behind the wall now. We're safe." Part of him was dying to give her a proper tour of the Land of Sweets. His parents had cut the tour short ten years ago, when they learned he'd snuck out. The people had danced for them, but he hadn't been able to show her all the wonders of his mother's kingdom.

He had been in so much trouble once she returned home.

"These trees look so different. Why is the bark so red?"

"That's because these are cinnamon trees." Klaus stopped Peppermint close to the edge of the path and peeled off a piece of reddish-brown bark. It flaked away, and he handed it to Clara. "Taste it."

She bit into it, and made a noise that brought to mind pleasures he had no business thinking about right now. Riding a horse in an aroused state was not comfortable.

"That's incredible!" Clara turned her face upwards, and he tried to see his country from her perspective. "Your country is amazing."

"You don't remember your last visit?"

She shrugged. "It was nighttime."

Peppermint walked toward the sunrise, which captivated her. "Your sky is purple! And the sun is... red?"

"Yes. What color is your sun?" He'd never seen daylight in the Realm of Waking and he was curious.

"It's yellow, of course."

"That seems so strange to me." Klaus couldn't imagine a world where the sun wasn't red.

"It's normal! Yellow sun, blue sky, and green grass."

"Blue sky? That's so odd!" At least they had green grass in common.

"It's true!" Clara's laugh rang through the cinnamon trees, her face lighting up with glee. Klaus's heart beat double-time as they came upon a bridge to cross the southern river.

"Why is your river yellow?" She asked, her nose wrinkled.

He chortled. "This is the Lemonade River."

"You're not serious."

"I'm absolutely serious. The Lemonade River sits to the south of the palace, and the Orange Juice River to the north." He pulled Pepper off to the side of the bridge once they'd crossed and dismounted. "I'll get us a drink while we're here." He knew he had a canteen in his saddle bag somewhere.

The look of consternation on her face amused him to no end. "Do you not drink water?"

"We have a river that is made of water as well. We call it the Sweet River."

"Is that because the water is sweet?"

"I'll let you decide that for yourself. Aren't you thirsty?"

"Well, yes…"

"I'll return in a moment."

Klaus bent and caught lemonade from the river below, then handed her the canteen. She lifted it to her lips and took a hesitant sip. "Mm, that's delicious."

"Drink your fill. There's plenty more where that came from." He watched her drink it down with enthusiasm.

With a shy dip of her head, she handed him an empty canteen, which he refilled for himself, and drank down. Peppermint also took advantage of the break, drinking straight from the river. When he'd had enough, Klaus made sure they had a full canteen for the rest of their trip, then mounted behind Clara once more.

As they headed towards the palace, she relaxed against him. He was enjoying the sensation of her weight leaning into his chest when she asked another question. "Who is the Sugar Plum Fairy?"

"That would be my mother."

"So, like a queen?"

He nodded. "Yes, but the title is different. The Sugar Plum Fairy rules the Land of Sweets, the Dew Drop Fairy rules the Land of Flowers, and the Snow Fairy rules the snow angels in the Land of Ice and Snow."

His companion was silent for a moment. "What of your father?"

"What of him?"

"Is he..." she bit her lip. "Is he dead?"

"No, why would you think that?"

"It's just... usually in my realm, the men rule. Only one country I know of has a queen right now."

Ah. He had a little knowledge of this from pestering his uncle about the Realm of Waking when he was a child. "Uncle Ludwig said yours was a patriarchal society. But my realm is matriarchal."

"What do you mean?"

"Well, for instance, we are usually ruled by women and not by men."

She sat up and gave him a strange look. "How come?"

Klaus shrugged. "It's always been that way. The women are the ones with magic. Except for Uncle Ludwig. And his is not very strong."

"Women have magic?"

"Yes, and so do you."

She tilted her head to one side, her eyes narrowed. "What do you mean?"

"The Mouse King has dark magic users at his beck and call. They changed his form and gave him immense power, but at the cost of his soul. Only strong light magic can defeat him, which you did. So clearly, you have magic."

Her brow furrowed in confusion. "Why is he a king, and not a queen?"

"Things have always run differently in the Land of the Animals. They have no natural magic, which is why the ones that gained it had to use... underhanded means."

"That sounds terrifying." She shrank back against his chest.

Klaus transferred the reins to one hand and wrapped an arm around Clara to comfort her. "That's why we need you. You were the only one to weaken him, and he stayed gone for years. But he's back and my parents don't seem to realize..." He hesitated to tell her.

"Realize what?"

"That it was you that defeated him and not me. They didn't believe me when I was younger about your shoe being the key thing that turned the tide."

She watched his face, silent. "No one believed you?"

He shook his head, unwilling to explain how his parents insisted a Waking couldn't have magic. Eventually, he'd stopped trying to convince them otherwise.

Her lashes kissed her cheekbones. "No one believed me either."

Averting his eyes, Klaus realized the quiet of the cinnamon woods was giving way to the clanging sound of pickaxes. Ah, the perfect distraction.

He urged Pepper into a trot, guiding him towards the mines. Clara looked around, then back at him. "What is this place?"

"The chocolate mines."

Her eyes bugged out. "Chocolate mines?"

"Yes, don't they have that in your world?"

"In my world, chocolate doesn't come from a mine."

The foreman, a stout dwarf with a ginger beard, hailed him from the entrance where miners were bringing rough chunks of chocolate out on carts and wheeling it away. "Greetings, My Prince. Come for a quality check?" The elder dwarf winked.

"If you please, Mr. Berg. A taste for each of us?" Klaus had come here often in his youth and counted the foreman as a friend.

Mr. Berg broke off two pieces of the next cart to come out of the mine and handed them up. Clara's eyes were wide. She took the smaller of the two and bit into it. "This is amazing."

"The dwarven miners have a good eye." Klaus popped his entire piece into his mouth and let the sweetness melt on his tongue. This one was strong, and a touch bitter, but still delicious.

"We hit a dark chocolate vein yesterday. It's excellent quality." The elder dwarf fidgeted, which was unlike him.

"Something on your mind?"

"Since you're here, Your Highness. Have you any word from the Land of Flowers?"

"I have not. Hopefully, the Dew Drop Fairy can get her people to safety. I'm sure my parents would offer refuge."

"If you hear anything, let me know. The dwarves will house refugees, as many as we can." Horace Berg was not only the foreman, but a leader among the dwarves. They often elected him as a spokesman for the community.

"Thank you, Mr. Berg. I'll pass the message along." He swallowed the last of the chocolate. "We must be off. Keep up the good work!"

Klaus turned Peppermint's head, then spoke to his companion. "What did you think?"

Clara finished her chocolate, and her dainty tongue licked the leftover from her fingers. "Delicious. I've only ever had chocolate in a cup."

"We mix it into a beverage sometimes, but most prefer it in its solid form." He guided Peppermint back onto the road.

"What are these stones? I saw something similar on the wall as well."

"Gingerbread. It's our most common building material. Very sturdy when done right."

She gasped. "Won't the mice just eat their way through?"

Klaus shrugged. "Not this gingerbread. It's impervious to pretty much anything we've thrown at it. And we glaze the walls so they're waterproof."

A comfortable silence descended as they made their way through the countryside. It was easy to forget the threat that lay beyond their borders. The Mouse King would bring darkness and permanent winter to his beloved land, and Klaus hated his parents hadn't moved to help the other countries.

They had been at peace for so long, no one remembered how to wage war. And the Mouse King had taken advantage.

The sun shone a light pink as it rose in the lavender sky when they arrived at the village that encircled the palace. A cow mooed from behind a fence of peeled cinnamon tree logs.

"I didn't realize you had cows here!"

"Of course! Cows, pigs, and chickens, too. Uncle Ludwig told me many centuries ago we used to trade with your realm and that's how we got our own farm animals." He patted Peppermint's neck with affection.

"You don't have animals here?"

"Not the same domesticated breeds you do."

He didn't dare stop now that they were this close to the palace. But Klaus found he was in no hurry to arrive, either. He kept Peppermint at a trot through the village. Clara took in the sights, still leaning against his shoulder.

She was an altogether different woman with him than she'd been around her family. And he hated the idea of sending her home to marry that swine. What could he do to convince her to stay once the threat was over?

Chapter 5

Houses made of gingerbread glazed to a shine stood on either side of the road. Cinnamon and other spices perfumed the air. Trees with curious, sugared fruits grew in yards and along fences made of cinnamon wood or peppermint sticks. Curious onlookers bowed and curtsied when the Prince's horse passed by.

They passed through a market full of brightly colored stalls with citizens selling their wares. Clara wished she had some coin to check out the local fare. After their all-night ordeal, she was hungry.

Klaus guided Peppermint around a fountain in the middle of the square, bursting with lemonade. More houses lay beyond it, and she took a closer look at the subjects.

There were short, stout dwarves, like the chocolate miners. And slender people with pointed ears and unnatural hair colors like pink, blue, and a bright orange. Their skin was tinged with the same color, but lighter.

"What race are your subjects?" she finally asked quietly.

"We have several. You've met the dwarves. The brightly colored ones are the pixies; they have wings but don't always use them. We also have nymphs, dryads in the woods, and other fae. Or fairies, if you're more familiar with that term."

"I thought they were all a myth!"

"As I mentioned, Uncle Ludwig said our realms used to trade a long, long time ago. But the veil between the worlds was drawn closed and can no longer be opened, except by a Master Tinkerer."

"A master what?"

"Tinkerer. It's a type of mage. Uncle Ludwig's mother was an extremely strong Tinkerer, and she passed some of her gift to him. How he can open portals is beyond me, but he can. Mother doesn't like him to do it often."

"Why is that?"

"Ever since the Realm of Waking entered the scientific age, magic stopped working there. So we have nothing to trade now. And they are not exactly kind to things they don't understand."

"What kind of fae are you?"

Klaus chuckled. "I'm a Nutcracker. Remember, we're the Land of Sweets *and* Toys."

"But your mother..."

"Sugar Plum Fairy is merely a title, because she rules the land of the sweet fae."

"I see." This was *such* a detailed dream. She could feel the heat of Klaus's chest at her back, had tasted the chocolate and lemonade.

Her heart sank when she thought about waking up and losing this alternate realm to the rising sun. She resolved to take in as much as she could, imprinting it on her mind so she could remember this dream. So she would never forget how it felt to have a handsome prince at her back.

She ground her molars as a lump rose in her throat, remembering her parents' betrayal. Even in her dreams, she couldn't escape it.

Tall, brown walls rose before her, studded with jewel-like candies. She craned her neck upward. A castle made of gingerbread, complete with towers and ramparts! Another portcullis of peppermint canes rose in front of them across a bridge over an orange moat. They must have brought in juice from the Orange Juice river that Klaus had mentioned. Wooden doors creaked as they opened outward.

Klaus's arm gripped her tighter. "What's wrong, Klaus?"

"I was afraid of this. I should have ridden straight here, before word got out." His gaze softened as he looked into her eyes. "But I can't regret taking the time to show you my homeland."

Her cheeks heated, and she dropped her gaze downward.

Their mount walked forward, crossing the bridge, to stand in front of the massive doors as they opened. Six soldiers in tall black hats, crimson pants, and black military coats marched on either side of a man and a woman.

Both were dark-haired and stood with a regal air. The woman bore a golden crown upon her head. Her pale rose gown sparkled in the sunlight, a sleeveless, strapless affair with a large bell-shaped skirt. This must be the Sugar Plum Fairy.

Klaus jumped from his horse and reached for Clara, helping her slide off the saddle. She was woefully underdressed to meet royalty! Still, she curtsied when he bowed.

"Mother, I can explain."

"And you will, son. Who is this?"

"Mother, Father, may I present Miss Clara Stahlbaum of the Realm of Waking. Clara, these are my parents, Galiena and Alaric von Süssland."

She curtsied again. "I'm honored, Your Majesties."

But the queen's voice grew icy. "We will discuss this inside. Come."

Klaus offered Clara his arm as a stable hand ran up and took the reins of his horse. "I'm sorry, my dear."

"What for?"

"For whatever is about to transpire."

They followed his parents inside the palace. Sugared windows let in the sunlight. Thick columns of peppermint canes created arches in the ceiling, with glazed gingerbread floors laid out in a swirling pattern. She didn't have time to admire the rich tapestries as they hurried through to what she had to assume was a private chamber.

Galiena led them to a study lined with bookshelves and smelling like rich cinnamon. She sat behind a desk and her consort pulled a chair up to the end of the desk, leaving the two in front of it for the prince and his guest.

She was dying to know what they made the fabric of the seat out of. It felt like a rich brocade. But how did they get that here?

At the queen's nod, the guard pulled the door shut, and Alaric locked it before sitting down. Before she bade them speak, Klaus's mother muttered some words Clara couldn't make out and spread her hands wide. The noise from outside the room was no more.

"A muffling shield, to be certain this goes nowhere else." The queen sat back in her chair and crossed her arms across her chest. "*What* were you thinking, Klaus?"

Klaus sighed and gripped the armrests of his chair. "That I knew who really defeated the Mouse King ten years ago, and that we need her to help us again."

Her brows drawn together, Klaus's mother turned to his father. "What do you think, my love?"

An older version of her Nutcracker Prince rubbed his bearded chin in thought. "I want to know how a Waking could have magic."

"As do I." Galiena eyed Klaus suspiciously, then turned to Clara, the look on her face causing her to shiver. She reminded her of her own mother when she was upset. "I don't recognize the Stahlbaum name. And she lives in the Realm of Waking. How can she have magic at all, let alone powerful enough to defeat the Mouse King?" She turned back to her son, as if Clara wasn't there.

"Not twelve hours ago, returning through the portal, a squad of mice attacked us. She threw up a shield, which allowed us to get away."

"Are you sure one of our Casters was not in the forest at the same time?"

Klaus scowled, but Clara knew the Sugar Plum Fairy was right. She wasn't of this realm, and what happened made little sense.

Why had she come here? She should have told him no, that she was going to bed. And now her beautiful dream was starting to feel more like a nightmare. Klaus looked down at her with desperate eyes. If he thought she had any idea how she'd done any of that, he was wrong.

She rubbed a hand over the spot in her chest where it ached. A dream couldn't give her magic powers. Which meant Klaus had put himself in danger for nothing. And he'd never look at her the way he had in the drawing room again.

Klaus told the story once more. His parents *had* to believe him this time. "Ten years ago, when the mice attacked me in the other realm, they caught Clara in the crossfire as well."

His guest wrinkled her brow. "But I thought they were attacking me."

He shook his head. "No, they were coming after me, trying to take advantage of your parents locking me up in that cabinet. They must have spied on Uncle Ludwig that night and known where to find me." Klaus turned back to his parents. "The Mouse King nearly had me, but Clara threw her shoe at him. That's what made him lose his magic. He turned into a small rodent and fled. His soldiers followed."

"Is this true?" The queen turned to Clara.

"Not exactly." She tugged at her cloak. "It was my house slipper."

Klaus smiled at her fondly. "Regardless," he continued. "Clara had magic then, and it's only grown stronger. We were followed to the Enchanted Forest, but she threw up a shield that let us get away."

Clara tugged at his sleeve. "Are you sure it wasn't the forest helping us earlier?"

"I'm sure. The Enchanted Forest must be asked, but you commanded. Besides, it would help the mice as soon as it would help us. It's a neutral zone."

"What did this shield look like?" The Sugar Plum Fairy rested her chin on her hand, her tone curious.

Clara licked her lips. "Like a wall made of white light, I guess?"

His mother tapped at her chin. "Very interesting." Just like that, Mother had decided. "We can always test her. Maybe magic from the Realm of Waking could be what defeated him."

When Clara opened her mouth to protest, Klaus shook his head. Let her think the magic was from a different realm. She'd find out soon enough that wasn't the case.

At least, he thought so.

"Mother, I'm afraid we'll need to put that off until later. Neither of us has slept since yesterday. She can't do magic with an empty well."

"Very well. She shall have the guest wing."

As the Sugar Plum Fairy led the way, he tried to give Clara a reassuring smile. She looked over her shoulder at him with wide eyes, and he rose to follow. Alaric went with him. If Mother noticed them trailing behind her, she said nothing.

Klaus's father grasped his shoulder, forcing him to follow the women at a distance. "Son, this doesn't excuse you for sneaking out of the castle with your uncle."

He fought to keep from rolling his eyes. "If we win the war, then it was worth it."

"You're not a child anymore. There is no excuse for such behavior."

"That's right, I'm not a child and therefore don't require a curfew."

Father shook his head. "You are still the prince of this land, and you have a target on your back every time you leave. What if the mice had captured you?"

Klaus breathed deeply in through his nostrils, his hands clasped behind him in agitation. "Please try to understand, Father. I knew there was a mage in the Realm of Waking. I watched her defeat the Mouse King once. And I know she can do it again."

Alaric shook his head. "And what if she can't?"

"Then at least we tried!" Klaus stopped as he raised his voice to the Sugar Plum Consort. The servants were staring. Frustration oozed from every pore. He faced his father and lowered his voice to a whisper. "Let Mother have her tested. There must be a reason she has magic. There *must*." Turning, he continued following his mother in silence.

Mother waved down the head housekeeper and spoke quickly in her ear just as Klaus caught up. Clara grasped onto his arm with a trembling hand, and he wanted to beat his own ass for bringing her here.

This woman had thought their realm a figment of her imagination. But when he asked for help, she agreed. And now his mother was treating her like some sort of suspicious character. He laid his hand over hers at his elbow with a gentle squeeze. She was so brave, his Clara.

They followed his mother's housekeeper to the guest wing of the palace. Thankfully, his parents left them. Klaus could have taken her there himself, but Mrs. Rein would have her own duties to fulfill.

"I'm sorry." Klaus spoke under his breath.

Clara shook her head, her face ashen. "It's not your fault. I chose to come with you."

"I did not know she'd be so…" Unwelcoming. Harsh. Klaus realized that he'd seen her be cold and unfeeling towards people who she distrusted before, but he'd never dreamed she'd be that way with his Clara.

And yes, he was referring to her as his. Back in his homeland, far away from the engagement that she said would be official in six days' time, he could pretend she was his. For a little while.

Outside the door to the guest suite, Mrs. Rein paused and opened the door for them. "Lady Clara," she curtsied, "please let us know if there's anything you require."

"Is there somewhere I might find a dress?" She winced. "There wasn't time to pack a trunk and I'm still in my nightclothes."

"I'll send Trixie right away. She can arrange it for you."

As Mrs. Rein left them so she could call for the maid to assist his guest, Klaus gestured for her to enter first.

"There's a sitting room here, and the bedroom and bath are behind that door."

She merely nodded, then sat gingerly on the crimson settee. He stood in front of her, unsure whether she wanted him to sit on the other side of the small sofa or if he should take the chair across from her.

"Are you alright?"

Clara took a deep breath, then whispered, "I'm scared, Klaus. What if it was all a fluke? Then you put yourself in danger for nothing."

"It was not for nothing." He slid onto the settee at her side. "I wanted to find you again, regardless. I'm only sorry about how my parents have treated you."

"Still, I don't know the first thing about war. Let's suppose I have magic. How am I going to help you defeat the Mouse King and his entire army in just a few days?"

"Leave the strategy to me and my father. Once you harness the power that I've seen you wield, we will determine the best tactics." As prince of the Land of Sweets and Toys, Klaus was familiar with carrying immense responsibility on his shoulders. It had been thrust on him essentially at birth, since he'd never had a sister to inherit the throne. She was struggling under his expectations, and Klaus cursed himself once more for thrusting her into this. If only he'd had more time to explain!

"I still don't... I just don't know, Klaus."

Dark circles had formed under her eyes. She needed rest, first and foremost. He'd have a meal sent up as soon as she was awake. And he could use a nap himself. He wouldn't be able to help carry her burden if he wasn't in tip-top shape. "One step at a time. Why don't you get some sleep?

Everything will look better after a nap. Then I can take you for a proper tour of my home."

She nodded, and he stood with her. "Thank you, Klaus."

His brow furrowed in confusion. "I'm not sure why you would thank me when I'm the reason you're in this mess."

She graced him with a small smile. "For listening. And for... believing in me." Then she did the most miraculous thing. Leaning in, she pressed a lingering kiss to his cheek. Klaus couldn't even breathe, scared to move and break the moment. His skin clung to the memory of her lips as she pulled away.

He couldn't look away from those soft chocolate eyes, drowning him in emotion. Without looking away, he pressed her knuckles to his lips. "Always."

After holding on a few moments longer than was probably proper, Klaus released her hand. "Whenever you wake, send for me."

Clara nodded. "I will."

"'Til then." He took one last look at her and then tore himself away and gently closed the door to the suite behind him.

Leaning back against the door, Klaus closed his eyes and breathed for a moment. Then he made his way to his own wing, back down the staircase and up another that would take him to his rooms on the other side of the palace. He should have talked to Uncle Ludwig ages ago about her magic. Surely, her own godfather would have an inkling of what was going on. Yet if he knew, he'd never mentioned it. As much as Klaus desired it, he doubted he could keep her. Even if her magic weren't a fluke, she wouldn't be allowed to stay in the Realm of Dreams.

Magic existed only in Dreamers. Legend spoke of rare Dreamer and Waking marriages, and that the descendants of those matches could inherit a parent's magic. Supposedly, some of them had moved to the Realm of Dreams before the portals closed. But his parents always told him those were just children's tales.

No one from the other realm could ever stay.

Chapter 6

Clara awoke bewildered several hours later. She was in a soft, large four-poster bed of a reddish-brown wood with fine linens. Looking around the room, she didn't recognize the wallpaper, a cream-colored affair decorated with beautiful golden scrollwork. A wardrobe of the same color as the bed frame stood off to one side of a window. Then, the events of the night before came back to her. She had gone to sleep and then woke up in her dream. Which meant she was still asleep.

How confusing!

Shaking her head, she rose when she heard a soft knock. That must be what had woken her. "One moment!" She smoothed her hair down, sure she looked a fright. Opening the bedroom door, she hurried across the sitting room. "Who is it?"

"It's Trixie, Miss."

She opened one of the two white doors and ushered in a small woman with short blue hair and blue tinted skin.

She wore a plain brown maid's gown and apron, like the housekeeper had earlier. That must be the uniform for servants here. Trixie pushed a cart with a dome on top, her head barely rising to the same height. She came only to Clara's waist. This had to be one of the pixie race Klaus had mentioned.

"His Highness asked Cook to send supper up for you. The Sugar Plum Fairy has arranged for your testing to happen tomorrow morning. I brought you some mage robes and a few other things to wear while you stay with us. They're in the wardrobe."

"Thank you very much, Trixie."

Trixie sat the cart in front of an armchair and waited for her to sit. Then she lifted the dome and set out silverware and a glass. Clara breathed a sigh of relief when the silverware looked perfectly normal.

"Would you like water, lemonade, or wine, Miss?"

"Lemonade would be wonderful." Trixie poured a glass of the liquid sunshine that she had tasted on the ride into town, then went to stand by the door.

"Won't you please sit?" At her hesitation, she continued. "Klaus is the only person I know in this entire realm, and I'm so curious about everything. I hate to pester him."

Trixie sat down gingerly on the settee across from her. "If that's what you wish, I will answer as many questions as I can, Miss." Clara nodded, then looked down at her plate.

"My name is Clara. Let's start with, what's for supper?" She tried a smile, and the little pixie returned it.

"In the center of your plate is a venison steak with a side of roasted tubers and carrots. Then there is a fairy cake topped with a gumdrop for dessert. Enjoy!"

The tubers reminded her of potatoes, but the carrots were purple. They must grow differently here under their odd sun. She cut into the steak and nearly moaned when the delicious meat hit her tongue. Silence descended as she ate ravenously, finishing the main entrée in minutes. The fairy cake was a small, single serving vanilla cake with decadent chocolate frosting and a strange red bulb on top. She plucked it off the cake, entranced. It was soft and covered in a fine sugar.

"What did you say this was, again?"

"A gumdrop, Miss Clara."

"Where do they come from? I've never seen one."

"Really? They grow on bushes here. There's an entire row in the palace gardens." Trixie's violet eyes were almost too large for her face. "That one is cherry flavored."

Cherry! She popped it into her mouth and immediately the sweetness burst on her tongue. Chewing slowly, she savored it. "That tastes better than any cherry I've ever had back home!"

Trixie giggled, then blushed. "My apologies, Miss. Your face was just so... well, your reaction was adorable, if I may."

Clara chuckled at herself. "I took no offense, Trixie. I've been thrust into this realm and I feel like a fish out of water." She didn't dare call it a dream, for fear of upsetting her companion. It was certainly real to its inhabitants.

"Is there anything else I can do for you? Would you like a bath, perhaps?"

Soaking off the grime of their trip through the forest sounded divine. "That would be lovely. But the prince wanted me to call for him when I woke up."

Trixie smoothed her dress as though she were nervous. "I'm sure he won't mind waiting for you to prepare. I'll get it ready while you finish up." With a flounce, the small pixie headed towards the bedroom door.

By the time she had finished dessert, Trixie had a warm bath drawn in the white clawfoot tub in the bathroom, whose wallpaper matched the bedroom. A toilet and sink stood in the corner. Of course, the palace of her dreams would have hot and cold running water.

Light blue flower petals floated in the water. A generous towel hung off a rack to the side. "Would you like your clothes washed, Miss Clara?"

"Yes, I'll leave them outside the door. Are there undergarments in the wardrobe?"

"Of course, Miss. I'll return when you're done."

Clara undressed as soon as she was alone, slipping her nightgown, robe, and chemise out into the bedroom. She held her hair out of the water as she sank in, splashing water on her face. Leaning back into the tub, she luxuriated in the water for several minutes. So much had happened.

This dream was amazing, from its lavender sky to the lemonade flowing through the ground. Which also produced chocolate of such a quality its people preferred to eat it in its natural state rather than sweeten it into a drink. While her mind whirled, she felt such a kinship with this place.

It made sense. Of course, a place created from her own imagination would feel more like her home than her parents' house. She rubbed over her limbs, then rose out of the tub and dried off. These were thoughts for later. There was a prince waiting for her.

Her prince. The one that had rescued her all those years ago in yet another silly dream. Seeing him transform had been incredible. And he cared for her. Her cheeks flushed when she recalled how he'd nearly kissed her in the drawing room. It had taken everything in her to pull away. She rubbed the towel vigorously over her aching heart. It wouldn't do to get attached to a dream when she had a fiancé waiting. Her whole life she'd known her sole purpose would be to marry well and produce children. That's why she'd spent so much time in the library, soaking it up while she could. But for now, instead of a book, this dream was her escape. If Papa hadn't promised her hand to Berengar, she might never wake up. To run out on an engagement was social suicide for the entire family, and Mama would never forgive her. Margareta Stahlbaum hated to be the center of gossip. Though she'd always known her mother didn't like her, Clara had never been so outright disloyal in her heart.

And yet, here she was. Wishing for a different family, a different last name. Anything to earn her freedom.

Why couldn't they have promised her to a man like Klaus? Someone who listened, who valued her, who made her feel beautiful?

But Nutcrackers didn't come to life and try to kiss you. This could only ever be a dream.

Besides, what Klaus really needed her for was to defeat the Mouse King. *If* she could reproduce what she'd done ten years ago. She still didn't know *why* she'd thrown her slipper. Just that it had worked.

True to her word, Trixie was waiting in the bedroom for Clara after her bath, next to the wardrobe and a vanity she hadn't noticed before. She had pulled the stool out in front of her.

Clutching the towel around her body, Clara padded over to the wardrobe, barefoot. "I think just a day dress for now. I don't expect any fancy dinners when I've already eaten."

Trixie nodded and pulled out what looked at first glance to be a simple red gown. That's when she noticed that besides the long-sleeved black robe in the wardrobe, all the gowns were just as fancy as her Christmas gown. "My goodness, are we expecting a party?"

"His Highness insisted you have the best available. Are they not to your satisfaction?"

"They're beautiful, but I normally only wear such gowns for special occasions."

The blue pixie grinned in amusement. "When you stay in the palace, a special occasion often surprises you." She held out a chemise for Clara, who dropped the towel and slid into it.

"You have very similar fashions to what I wore back home."

"Master Ludwig advised us what you're accustomed to wearing. He didn't think you'd appreciate something like what Her Majesty wears."

"I'll have to thank him later."

Once she was laced into the stays and gown, Trixie gestured to the stool in front of the vanity. When Clara sat down, she began to brush. "What do you usually do with your hair?"

"Heidi helps me." She explained the process of braiding the front sections of her hair and coiling the back section up onto the back of her head. Trixie furrowed her blue brows.

"Very well. I want you to concentrate on that style for me, Miss Clara. Hopefully, I'll get it right." Then her violet eyes glowed, as she muttered something under her breath, and her long blonde hair lifted and styled itself!

When Trixie's eyes stopped glowing, Clara's hair was finished. "That was incredible!"

Her blue cheeks turned a pinkish hue. "My pleasure. Now, I'm sure the prince is waiting for your summons. I'll send him to you."

Klaus hurried up the hallway. It was evening, and the sun had started to set, but he was eager to show Clara around. She'd have an early morning start, and he didn't want to keep her up too late.

At the double doors that led to the guest suite, he gave his breathing a chance to slow. Then he reached out and knocked three times on the door. Almost immediately it opened, and the vision of Clara in a scarlet gown stole his breath clean away. In the back of his mind was the vague notion that her dress matched his coat, and they would look like a couple strolling through the palace gardens. But her beauty eclipsed all thought.

"Your Highness."

He shook his head. "Please don't, Clara. You're not my subject."

She blushed. "Very well, Klaus."

He raised her fingers to his lips and kissed them gently, as if they'd been separated for months. "I thought perhaps I dreamed you up. That when I woke up, you would still be in your realm."

Clara's brow furrowed. "You thought *you* dreamed *me*?"

He tucked her hand into the crook of his arm and led her down the hall. "Perhaps I should pinch myself, just in case." Her giggle made him grin.

Watching her face take in the grand staircase and the hall below, Klaus wondered what to show her first.

"That staircase over there," he pointed to the far side of the wall as they descended, "leads to my parents' wing. That's where my rooms are as well."

They reached the bottom of the staircase and their shoes clicked on the gingerbread floor. Clara pulled on his arm towards a tapestry.

"I wanted to see these earlier, but we didn't have time." Her brown eyes swept over the image. "Isn't that your mother?"

"Yes, the Dew Drop Fairy had this commissioned as a coronation gift. It shows the three queens of the realm. They're all childhood friends." He couldn't keep the sadness from his voice as he pointed out his aunts immortalized in thread. "The one in green is the Dew Drop Fairy, my Aunt Lorelei. And the woman with white hair and the moon crown is Aunt Crescentia, the Snow Queen."

She turned to him, worry written all over her face. "Are your aunts well?"

"No one's heard from Aunt Lorelei since the Mouse King invaded Blumenland. And Schneeland has been under siege for quite some time. Aunt Crescentia is a powerful mage whose family specialty is defensive spells; she's kept the Mouse King out, but also everyone else. The Land of Snow and Ice might as well have fallen with the Land of Flowers." A sour taste rose in the back of his mouth, even as he uttered the words. His plan to bring Clara into the fold had been a last-ditch effort to free his realm; without her, he feared all hope was lost.

The red light of sunset filtered through the windows, and he knew time grew short. "Let me show you the throne room and the ballroom."

"I'd really love to see the gardens." Her words came out in a rush. "Trixie told me about some things you grow there. Could we see those first?"

Her excitement was adorable. "Of course. I can point out the others on the way."

They passed through the castle in record time, Klaus pointing certain rooms out as they strolled along. The servants must have all retired for the night, or were keeping out of the way, because they had the palace to themselves. She marveled over the candy jewels framing the door to where his parents held court, admired the tapestries that depicted moments from history. The huge dining hall where he said, "This is where you'll find us for breakfast tomorrow."

"Thank you for sending supper up for me. It was very thoughtful."

Klaus slowed his steps as he approached the courtyard that led to the gardens. "I wanted to introduce you to my world slowly. I have thrown you into a mad situation and I don't understand how you're not begging me to take you home."

"It's strange." Clara paused outside the door. "I know you say I've been here before, although the memory of it is foggy. But I feel more at home here than I do in my realm." She looked up at him and searched his eyes. "Isn't that strange?"

"Perhaps. Perhaps not." Could it be that she was part Dreamer? Or that the Realm of Dreams had accepted her?

Would she be the first to stay?

Klaus pushed those thoughts away as he took Clara through the courtyard. It was a wide-open lawn, cut with meandering paths and decorated with topiaries shaped to look like subjects of the land. Two Nutcracker soldiers flanked the door. A dwarf stood in the corner and pixies flitted about, all carved from the hedge.

"This is beautiful," She remarked.

"The orchard and gardens are along this path." He pointed at the central line of gingerbread pavers. "You want to see where we grow the food?"

"Yes, it's fascinating."

The pale blue moons lifted into the sky, and floating orbs of light followed as they strolled through the courtyard. The magic lit their path through the orchard first.

"What are all these?"

"These are sugar plum trees. They're native to this land, and where the Sugar Plum Fairy title originated."

Clara gazed up at the fruit in awe.

"Would you like one? There's a few that are ripe."

She looked back at him, frowning. "Is that allowed?"

He checked the pathway in both directions, then leaned forward and whispered, "Do you see anyone to tattle on us?"

Shaking her head, she smirked. He reached for a yellow one right above her head, then handed it to her.

"How do you know they're ripe?"

"The bright color is the final stage," he answered as she popped the sweet seed into her mouth and groaned.

"I love these, but they're so hard to find back home."

"Do you not grow many sweets?"

He waited while she formed words around the hard morsel.

"We grow sugar, but that's all. Things like sugar plums have to be made by hand."

"Really?" Klaus wondered how they'd mimicked his country's native fruit.

Clara nodded, then shook her head when he tried to pick another. "Mother always says I eat too many sweets."

"Nonsense," Klaus scoffed. "Sweets are our lifeblood. If a Dreamer doesn't get enough, they get sick!" He grinned when her eyes grew wide, then sobered. If only she could stay here.

"If a human eats too many sweets, she gets *fat*." She spat the word out as though it were dirty, her chin dropping to her chest as she looked away.

Gently, Klaus lifted her face to look him in the eye. He couldn't bear to see this beautiful creature think poorly of herself. "You're perfect just the way you are." His breath caught at the vulnerability in her eyes. The moment hung suspended in time as the magic orbs floated lazily around them, bobbing up and down.

He caught himself starting to lean in, then remembered he shouldn't kiss her. Clearing his throat, Klaus forced himself to break the moment. "Was there anything else you wanted to see?"

Clara gave herself a small shake. "There was… something on the fairy cake at supper tonight — Trixie called it a gumdrop? I had never seen them before!"

"Ah, the gumdrop and jellybean bushes are down this way."

"Jellybean? What is that?"

"It's another sweet. It's like a gumdrop but smaller, with a smooth shell."

He led her on a tasting tour of the gardens, past the bushes of lemon drops and the fallow candy corn fields. The chocolate limes and oranges blew her mind, although she was full by the time they arrived at that part of the orchard. So he ate most of those, feeding her a section of each.

"Are those cotton plants? In a garden?"

"Not quite," Klaus said as he plucked a tiny, pale blue puff of sugar and popped it in his mouth. "It's candy floss."

Loaded up on sugar, they meandered back to the court-yard, hand in hand. "The plants in this section are native to the Land of Flowers. We transplanted them generations ago."

Then Clara pointed out the bench under the arbor. "My legs are quite tired after all that walking. Shall we sit?"

Klaus hesitated, yet he realized asking was necessary. "Are you sure you want to sit there?"

"Why wouldn't I?" Apparently feeling bold, Clara let go of his hand and sank down beneath the greenery.

He stepped forward, drinking in the sight of those luscious curves, her plump pink lips, her blonde hair. Klaus sat down next to her on the bench, the mischievous, selfish side of him not saying another word, just pointing up at the mistletoe hanging above them. "That's why."

Her pale throat extended as she looked upwards. "Oh."

He licked his suddenly dry lips, lifting a clammy hand to brush her cheek with the backs of his fingers. "Do you remember... our first?"

Clara's pupils dilated, her voice breathy when she whispered, "Yes."

"But you thought it was a dream."

Her eyelashes kissed her cheekbones. "Yes."

"I — I'd like to do it again."

She blushed a pretty pink, her gaze falling to the ground once more. "It's bad luck not to, right?"

He slid so close he could feel the heat of her thigh even through their several layers of clothes.

"First, I'd like to tell you a story."

Chapter 7

"My people have a legend about the goddess that created our realm. Asteria, our Mother Goddess, fell in love with a god named Arus. But he was the God of the Underworld, and she was the goddess of life. They could only see each other from afar. Asteria and Arus thought they could never be together.

"However, as the goddess of life, all of creation could communicate with her. The little mistletoe vine spoke to Asteria and told her it would protect her in the underworld if she wore it in a crown while she visited with Arus.

"In thanks, she blessed the mistletoe plant and declared it would mark true love forevermore. So that's why we kiss underneath it. If your first kiss happens under the mistletoe, my people believe that it's a sign you're meant to be with that person." Klaus rubbed his lips together before he spoke again. "I've only ever kissed one person like that."

Relief and warmth flooded Clara's chest, and her voice came out in a squeak. "Me as well."

His fingers kept stroking her cheek, and she nearly purred like a cat. "Clara, may I..."

She craved his kiss so much it pained her. Engagement be damned. "*Please.*"

He brought his other hand up to cup her face, his gaze sweeping over her countenance. Memorizing her as she also committed his handsome face to memory. The orbs that had followed them through the gardens circled around them, giving off just enough light. As her prince leaned in, she closed her eyes, and he tentatively pressed his lips to hers.

Just like the first time, a tingle erupted from her mouth and spread to other parts of her. Klaus must have felt it too, because his hands dropped from her face, and he wrapped her in a tight embrace. Clara grasped at his jacket, her arms around his waist. His tongue brushed her lip, igniting something deep within her she'd never felt before, and she gasped. When his tongue slid along hers, their passions inflamed further, and before she knew it, she was panting for air as Klaus rained more kisses upon her lips. How long they sat there under the mistletoe she couldn't say, but when they parted, he pressed his forehead to hers as they breathed each other in.

"Worth the wait," he rasped.

"It was."

They stayed pressed together on that bench for some time. His blue eyes filled with longing as he unwrapped her arms from around him, holding her hands in his as he rose to his feet. "I should let you get some rest. Tomorrow is a big day."

Clara didn't want to rest. She wanted to keep kissing him. To keep ignoring that this dream would end. Resigned, she stood as well, pressing her thighs together at the ache between her legs. Who was this wanton creature? It must be Klaus that caused this reaction. She'd heard about feelings of passion and lust from her married friends, but never experienced it herself. 'Twas a shame it only happened to her in a dream.

They strode back to the guest wing in silence; the orbs following them as far as the castle door. Clara pondered Klaus's story. Could it be true that she'd only had these feelings for him, and him for her, because of a plant? Or was the moral of the story that the plant was just a messenger of fate?

Outside the tall white pair of doors that led to her rooms, Klaus kissed her once more, his lips lingering on hers. "Clara…"

"Yes?"

"I wish you could stay."

That threw a cold bucket of water on her thoughts. "I know." Even Klaus knew this was a dream. At some point Clara would wake up and be forced to return to the real world. She slid out of his embrace and opened the door. "I'll see you tomorrow. Good night, Klaus."

"Sweet dreams, lovely."

His gaze never left hers as she shut the door. Leaning against it, she waited for his footsteps. It took ages, but she finally heard him leave. Then she breathed a sigh of relief.

As she prepared for bed, wrestling with the ties to her corset, she thought about what he'd said. Could she abandon her duty to her family to stay in this Realm of Dreams?

The von Galens were a prominent family, and good friends with the Stahlbaums. Berengar was the eldest son, set to inherit the barony from his father. Mama would tell her tying the two families together would strengthen them.

Inwardly, Clara groaned. She'd be expected to produce *children* with the foul Berengar. And no matter what Mama promised her, she would never love him like her parents loved each other. His leers made her feel dirty, and she couldn't bear his condescending tone. She was sick just thinking about it.

On the other hand, Klaus made her feel beautiful and valued. He'd been so concerned for her well-being and comfort. *You are far more important to me than a horse.* She couldn't see her own brother saying such a thing, much less his best friend and cohort.

But a broken engagement would bring shame to her parents. Their friends and acquaintances might think their daughter unmanageable. Yet spinsterhood sounded far better than a miserable marriage to a man she despised. And her parents would need someone to care for them, eventually. As an unmarried woman, that would fall to her. The more she thought about it, the more she preferred that scenario to the first. She could make that trade.

Climbing into bed, Clara came to a decision. No matter how things turned out here, she would tell her parents she could not marry Berengar when she awoke. They wouldn't be happy about it, but she would rather disappoint than humiliate them. That meant she'd better talk to Mama and Papa before the New Year's Eve party. That way, only the two families would know about the broken engagement.

As she closed her eyes, she prayed to carry her memories of this dream for the rest of her life.

Clara faced the beautiful Galiena in the center of a large, empty room with ceilings higher than any cathedral she'd ever entered back home. An inch of sand covered the floor. "Has my son discussed the attributes of magic in our world?"

"A few, Your Majesty."

"And what did he tell you?" Galiena cocked her head to the side, her dark eyes watching Clara.

She tried desperately not to fidget under her sharp gaze. "That it's mostly women who have magic. But he also mentioned Godfather Drosselmeyer has some; that's why he can pass between worlds."

The Sugar Plum Fairy's eyes narrowed. "You know Ludwig?"

Clara nodded. Galiena hummed.

"Yes, Ludwig is what we call a Tinkerer. There are three classes of light mage. Tinkerers, Casters, and Healers. I can already tell you are not a Tinkerer. They always have violet eyes."

Her jaw dropped. "But Godfather —"

"— wears an eyepatch in the Realm of Waking, does he not?" Galiena said knowingly.

Stunned, she nodded.

"That is to cover up the sign of his magic. His mother was an extremely strong Tinkerer, and she passed her gift to him. If you see him while you're here, you'll understand."

Clara lowered her eyes at the reminder that this was all a dream.

"Now…" Galiena paced while she lectured. Clara turned to keep her in sight. "Healers are self-explanatory. Casters might sound odd, but that's what we call mages who have battle magic."

"Battle magic?"

"Yes. They can cast attacks or defensive spells. Based on what Klaus told me, if you have magic, you're a Caster."

That made sense.

"Now tell me what went through your mind when you threw a *slipper* at a seven-headed mouse."

Drawing in a deep breath, she tried to recall the strange dream. "My brother's hussars had come to life to help my Nutcracker — err, Klaus, but the mice had surrounded us. He shielded me, but I didn't want to keep running. I wanted to help, but I've never even held a sword before."

She blushed in embarrassment. "Women of my station aren't permitted to fight."

Galiena nodded. "Go on."

"So, I took my slipper off and prayed, then threw it with all my strength at the Mouse King."

The Sugar Plum Fairy's eyes narrowed. "What did you pray?"

Goodness, it had been so long ago, and a dream, even! "I'm not sure. 'Please save us' or something similar?"

Galiena raised her eyebrow, and Clara had the distinct sense that the Sugar Plum Fairy didn't believe her.

"No, I think it was, 'Leave us alone.'" That sounded better.

The Sugar Plum Fairy shook her head, then motioned to someone behind Clara she couldn't see. "Begin the test."

The hair at the back of her neck rose in the air. She'd known Klaus and his father were watching, but now she was aware of another presence. Was that magic? Or just her instincts?

A ball of ruby heat flew over her shoulder and erupted where Galiena had stood moments before. Gasping, Clara spun around, her black mage robe twirling behind her. A ball of fire burned out in the sand before her eyes. She reached up and touched her shoulder where the missile had grazed her. The stench of singed fabric assaulted her nostrils. And the heat from her robe...

A woman in purple mage robes and short, ginger hair lowered her hand. "Never take your eyes off your opponent!"

"Who are you?"

"That's not important right now. What's important is this!" Another red flare flew from her hand, straight towards her.

Heart racing, she ran out of the way. "I... I don't understand."

The strange woman growled. "Fight back!"

She wanted to, desperately, but she didn't know how! Balls of fire rained down on Clara, everywhere she turned. The heat and the physical evidence somehow shattered her belief that she was still dreaming. The Realm of Dreams was not a figment of her imagination. And she was in *actual* danger!

She faintly heard Klaus bellowing in the distance as her legs galloped over the sand-covered floor. "Stop this at once!"

The attacks paused, and Clara looked up in horror as her attacker loosed a volley toward the sky. The red-haired mage could control them like that? She found herself backed up against a pillar, dozens of the missiles streaking towards her from the ceiling. But that wasn't all.

Klaus took advantage of the lull and raced from the gallery toward her. No! What could he do against such an onslaught? He wasn't even wearing his sword!

A whistling noise assaulted her ears as the flares fell back to Earth. Her instincts took over and made a last-ditch attempt to gain control over this dream.

"Stop!" Her cry erupted from her chest, vibrating down to her toes. Down to the ground, to the center of the planet, and then back up through the soles of her feet and back out through her extended arms. The white light eclipsed her and Klaus both just as he reached her, forming a dome overhead that the red missiles exploded against, leaving them unharmed.

She heard nothing except her labored breathing. Klaus didn't even look like he'd broken a sweat. He just stared at her in awe, then a blinding grin spread out over his face as a slow clap broke the silence.

"Well done, lovely," He told her. "You impressed Mother Gingerbread."

Clara was still reeling from her revelation. "Mother who?"

"Take your shield down, young Caster." The mage, or Mother Gingerbread, was walking across the training facility towards them.

"Um... how?"

"Breathe deep, and relax. The shield will go down once your emotions are calm."

She did as she was told, and the white light dissipated. Mother Gingerbread then walked up behind Klaus and cuffed him across the head.

"Ow!"

"You know better than to interrupt a test, My Prince."

"Yes, ma'am."

Clara scowled at him as well. "You scared me!" He could have been seriously injured! It wasn't a dream!

That's when it finally hit her. This was *real*.

His jaw shifted, and he couldn't meet her gaze. "I'm sorry, Clara. I was scared, too."

"Well, now that's done." Mother Gingerbread ended the conversation and put her hands on her hips, then extended one to Clara. "Zelda Gingerbread, head mage. But since I train all the Casters, they started calling me Mother Gingerbread a long time ago."

"Clara Stahlbaum." She shook the proffered hand as if she were a marionette on a string.

"Are you alright?" Concern marred her Nutcracker Prince's face.

"It... I'm really not dreaming?"

His brow furrowed. "You didn't believe me?"

Shivers wracked her frame. "It... it all seemed... so... fantastic!"

Klaus's shoulders slumped. "You don't think I'm real?"

"Klaus, no..." Her hands twitched to reach out to him, but now Clara wasn't sure what the proper etiquette was. "I... wanted, very much, for you to be real. I thought if I played along, then I would remember the dream when I woke up..."

He gave her a tight smile, and she knew she'd disappointed him. That would not do! She rushed to hug him, her eyes damp. "I'm so sorry. You were so wonderful. I thought I was dreaming. I've never met anyone like you." When he wrapped his arms around her, forgiveness clung to her like a cloak.

"No, I should be the one apologizing. Everything happened so quickly, I didn't realize... Of course you wouldn't take me seriously. How could you, when you'd been told the last time was all a dream?" His hand rubbed soothing circles on her back. "I grew up knowing about your realm, but you didn't know about mine."

Klaus withdrew his arms and gathered her hands into his. "Please don't cry. It's alright, Clara. Everything is fine."

She drew a deep breath and nodded. "Thank you." She looked around the room, seeing it for the first time all over again. Klaus and his amazing realm were all *real*.

Which meant he had truly kissed her last night.

A throat cleared when Galiena joined them then, her expression unreadable. "So. it appears my son actually found a Caster in the Realm of Waking."

"Impossible." Mother Gingerbread turned to her queen in shock. "The veil was closed ages ago!"

"And yet..." The Sugar Plum Fairy gestured to Clara. "That's where she's from."

Clara drew Mother Gingerbread's attention back to her when she responded. "She's right. I'm not from this realm." Realm. It would take time to fully wrap her mind around the fact that she actually ended up in another world. But there would be time for that later.

Mother Gingerbread squinted, drawing up close to Clara's face as if she could see right into her soul. "Who are your parents?"

"Friedrich and Margareta Stahlbaum, ma'am."

The mage shook her head. "I don't know them."

"Apparently, Ludwig does." Galiena's arms crossed as she, too, studied her thoughtfully. Pressing a finger to her chin, she nodded at Mother Gingerbread. "She needs trained, and quickly. That shield was raised on instinct." To Clara, she said, "Are you ready to learn exactly how to control this?"

She nodded rapidly. "Yes, Your Majesty." The power she'd pulled still pulsed inside her, wild and untamed. She needed to train it, to understand it, so she could use it to help defeat the Mouse King. No wonder she'd never fit in back home!

"Come, Klaus. They have a *lot* of work to do, and not much time to do it. We must discuss some things with your father."

Her prince swallowed hard, and Clara wanted to memorize his look of wonder. No one had ever looked at her like that before. A surge of disappointment flooded her heart. Because once she returned home, no one ever would again.

Chapter 8

Despite knowing his presence would only distract Clara from her training, Klaus dragged his feet leaving the arena. His mother waited for him outside the door, her plum-colored cloak pulled tight around a sapphire gown. As they strode over the snow-speckled ground between the training facility and the main palace, Galiena surprised him.

"Son, I owe you an apology."

Klaus nearly tripped over his own boots. "Whatever for, Mother?"

"For not believing you about Clara. I didn't think it was possible, but she has magic, just as you said."

Klaus racked his brain, trying to remember when the queen had apologized to him last, and came up empty. "But you believe me now?" At last! His cheeks hurt from smiling as the adrenaline rushed through him. For a decade Klaus had swallowed the wound to his pride when his parents had insisted he made up the story from his youth. Finally, they had seen the truth.

"How could I not? Not only did I witness her throwing a shield, but she also did it to protect my idiot son."

He rolled his eyes. Fine, he had that coming. It had been a stupid move to run out onto the field to protect her, but he hadn't been able to stand by and watch a moment longer.

Insane? Yes. But he'd actually done them a favor. The Sugar Plum Fairy and her head mage did not know how selfless Clara could be. Klaus didn't think she'd have put the shield up to save herself. That's why he had run out, so he could protect her. That's what couples, like his parents, did for each other.

Gingersnaps. There he went, thinking of her in a way he had no right to. She was still engaged to Berengar.

But he'd never apologize for kissing her in the courtyard last night. Even now, his lips tingled at the memory. And other parts of him stiffened at the reminder of her lips against his.

He cut off that line of thinking as they arrived at the war room. Someone had hastily dusted off a long table with chairs around it, the map at the far wall glowing with the spell cast to bring it into existence. Alaric stood in front of it in a conversation with a dark-haired dwarf Klaus didn't recognize. Turning, the Sugar Plum Consort nodded to his wife and son.

"That will be all, Heinrich. Return to your post." The dwarf bowed to his father, then to his mother and himself, and left the room.

"What did the spy network say, Alaric?"

Spies! Of course, his parents had sent the court spies to infiltrate the Mouse King's lands. Klaus had criticized them for not moving against their enemy. He ought to have recognized that they would not remain passive while their beloved friends suffered.

Alaric cleared his throat and gestured at the map. Tiny red dots gathered along the border of the Land of Flowers.

"We have reports that the Mouse King is preparing to mount an attack from Blumenland. He must assume we would not expect it from the Dew Drop Fairy's side."

Galiena huffed and shook her head. "Does he think we live under rock candy? We know the Land of Flowers is under his control."

His father shrugged. "I don't pretend to know why he does the things he does. The spies said they'll be ready to move in two days' time."

"Then we have to attack tomorrow." Klaus jumped into the conversation. "Let's catch them unawares."

Alaric nodded. "That's sound. But Clara won't be fully trained by then."

Klaus scowled. How much training could a Caster do in one day? Had his trip to the Realm of Waking all been for naught?

Galiena laid a hand on his shoulder. "I'll talk to Zelda tonight. If she thinks Clara can help, then take her."

He shrugged, realizing more and more how haphazard this last-ditch effort to save his people had been. "It's not like we would have had a lot of time to train her, anyway."

"Half the training of Casters is babysitting." His mother gave him a rare grin. "Usually powers manifest in puberty and teenagers are a mess of hormones. She has an advantage here, coming into her powers as an adult."

"But she came into them ten years ago, remember?"

Galiena shook her head. "Not truly. The Realm of Waking dampens magic, even that of full-blooded Dreamers. She needed to be here for her powers to fully manifest. Had she thrown that spell at the Mouse King in our world, he likely would have died."

Klaus's heart pounded as his mother's words washed over him. This could have all been over ten years ago. There would have been a magnificent celebration across the realm. But then Clara would have returned home, and he'd never have an excuse to see her again.

Ironically, he found himself grateful that had not been the last battle.

Tomorrow wouldn't be, either, but they would turn the tide and *then* crush the Mouse King.

Alaric started speaking again, and using the spelled stylus to draw out his plan on the magical map. Uncle Ludwig had fashioned it himself so that anyone could use it, not just mages. "Take a platoon of soldiers and mages to the caves tomorrow. It cuts the distance by days. You must sneak up on the mouse camp after darkness falls. They'll be sluggish after their evening meal. Attack then, and our borders will be safe."

Klaus hadn't thought about using the passage to their neighbor. Since their discovery, the caves helped Dreamers transport goods between the Land of Sweets and the Land of Flowers.

"What if the mice know of the caves?"

Galiena shook her head. "When Ferdinand started raising his army, I met with Lorelei and Crescentia. Lorelei and I agreed if they ever invaded us, we'd spell the caves shut. You'll need Mage Gingerbread to break through. She is the only one besides me that knows the counter-spell."

"Aren't you coming, Father?"

Alaric shook his head. "Someone has to stay behind to command the guards along the border wall. And you're ready for this, son. I can't express how sorry I am that I didn't listen to you earlier. If I'd sent Ludwig, we could have given Clara more time to train."

Holy mistletoe. His parents were actually *trusting* him now. A weight lifted off his shoulders, light and warmth filling his chest. Now it was up to Klaus to prove he was worthy of that trust.

Their plan was sound. Klaus sent word to the generals that they were attacking the mice tomorrow. While their newest Caster learned how to harness her magic, he would inspect the troops and put them through their paces. The same as his father always did as Sugar Plum Consort.

Briefly, he let his mind wander to Clara. Her kind heart and fierce spirit would make a fine Sugar Plum Fairy, if his mother would permit her to stay. The beginnings of a plan of his own formed. Once the Mouse King was dead, he would petition for her to be the first Waking to be naturalized as a Dreamer. With their enemy gone, there was no way his parents would deny his request. The power he'd witnessed as a teen had to be only a fraction of her abilities, and he was more certain than ever that she was the key to taking down the tailed tyrant.

And frankly, her magic *proved* she didn't belong in the Realm of Waking with the man her parents had promised her to. She belonged with the Dreamers. She belonged with *him*.

Mother Gingerbread was a harsh taskmistress, running Clara through a gauntlet of mental and physical exercises. By lunch time, she was drenched in sweat, her energy stores depleted. But she could throw the magical missiles and shield on command. After lunch, the head mage had told her they would go over the more complicated spell work; she'd need to take notes until she memorized the incantations, but she was ready for battle with just those simple skills.

In her books, there was always a princess in hiding or an orphan with untapped magic. Clara had seemingly stumbled into a situation straight out of a fairy tale. Learning to access her magic had been liberating. Back home, she constantly felt powerless, forced to do what others expected of her. But with this *power* surging through her veins, she had clarity and purpose. A way to protect herself and others if necessary.

It was addicting.

The kitchen sent out a delicious meal of hearty stew along with crusty bread for dipping. She'd eaten her fill while Mother Gingerbread had gone inside to speak with the Sugar Plum Fairy. Clara tucked her extra piece of bread in her robe pocket and wandered the grounds, looking for the kitchen entrance, so she could take her dishes inside.

A side door stood open, rustling sounds coming from inside. Perhaps that was the way back to the kitchens?

She stepped across the threshold and stopped dead in her tracks. This wasn't the kitchen. It was the storeroom for the palace. Sacks of grain, flour, and vegetables adorned the neatly organized shelves alongside jars of various candies she'd seen around the realm. But there was no one here. Had the staff been so busy they had forgotten to shut the door?

It was then she heard a tiny, high-pitched squeak. Just once. Then twice. When it turned into a constant wail, Clara clapped her hands over her ears and followed the noise. A second squeaking joined the first, and she broke out into a run to the back of the storeroom.

Had the mice invaded?

With her new magic at her fingertips, she slid to a stop with a ball of crimson light hovering above her palm. In the corner was exactly what she'd feared.

A mouse the size of a man had snuck into the palace!

A mouse who hid in the corner like the coward he was.

A mouse that was... nursing a baby?

The creature in the corner wasn't a "he" at all. It was a "she." And *she was a mother*.

Clara swallowed against the lump in her throat, as the mouse shielded her baby from attack with her arms. Snuffing out the magic, she plunged them back into darkness, although just enough sunlight reached through the open door for her to see. The mouse raised her trembling head.

"What kind of king sends a spy with a baby?"

"I'm not a spy!" The mouse shook her head, violently denying the accusation. Human language sounded incredibly squeaky coming from her, but Clara could understand her.

"Then what are you doing here?"

"Looking for food." She looked down her long nose at the baby in her arms and drew her tattered dress back up over her chest. It was hardly more than a rag, dirty and patched. The baby mouse turned its head to look up at the interloper, his wide eyes taking everything in from where he was wrapped against his mother.

An ache formed in Clara's chest, but she wasn't sure what to do. How could she be sure the mouse wasn't a spy?

"So you're a thief then."

The female mouse hung her head. "I have no choice," she squeaked out. "The King called all the males to fight. My mate left for the war. There's been no food for us."

"Why would you come all this way if not to spy for your king?"

The mouse glared at her, then turned her head and spit. "He doesn't care about us. I'd never help him."

Wheels started turning in her head. "Is everyone back home hungry?"

Miss Mouse shrugged, cautiously eyeing her as she rose to her bare feet. "Most." She shuffled, her hands wringing her tail. "I'm sorry. I'll go now." Her eyes flitted from Clara to the door.

"Promise me you won't come back." Most people of this land would probably shoot her on sight and ask questions later. There was no sense in orphaning an innocent child, mouse or no.

Miss Mouse nodded. "Promise."

She dug into her pocket and held out the piece of bread she had left from lunch. "I'm sorry, it's not much, but take this."

Her companion squeaked as if she couldn't contain it, then took the food and clutched it to her chest. Tears fell from her big black eyes, and she bowed deeply.

"T-thank you."

"You're welcome. Now let's get you out of here."

At her nod, Clara led Miss Mouse back to the door and checked for anyone who might see her. No one was outside, but she could hear Mage Gingerbread calling her name.

"Be safe!" she whispered to the mouse and ran towards her trainer's voice. Time to go back to her lessons.

Even after she returned to the training grounds, she couldn't get the image of the poor, terrified mouse out of her head.

She rounded the corner and nearly ran into Mother Gingerbread. "I'm so sorry, Head Mage. I was trying to find the kitchen so I could return my dishes."

A pink-tinted pixie in the brown servant's uniform bowed next to the mage. "Let me take them for you, Miss." He slipped the dishes out of her hands and trotted back to the palace.

Mother Gingerbread nodded and resumed the lesson.

"Sometimes, you will need to infuse an object with your magic, instead of just hurling it as a missile. I will demonstrate with this spear."

Clara tried to focus, but the injustice haunted her. The Mouse King's people were starving while he waged war? He didn't even care about his own subjects! All he wanted to do was spread darkness and misery, and to what end?

This was why Klaus had brought her in. They *must* defeat the Mouse King once and for all. Something told her that very few would mourn him.

That afternoon, she trained with the other Casters before a servant brought word that there was to be a banquet that night. She returned to her rooms, where Trixie had run her a bath, then helped her choose an elaborate gown and did her hair up like the Sugar Plum Fairy kept hers. It showcased her ears and drew the eye to her neck. Trixie assured her the style was acceptable here, despite the scandal it would have caused back home. Thankfully, the gown was no less modest. This one was a rich sapphire blue silk trimmed in ivory lace. A bow of matching ribbon adorned the neckline with a snowflake broach.

"You look stunning, Miss Clara!" Trixie tittered, clearly pleased with herself.

"Thank you, Trixie."

"Our prince is going to have his hands full."

"What do you mean?"

"You watch. He's going to have to fight off every man at the banquet. If he's not in a duel tomorrow at dawn, I'll eat my wings."

Clara sighed, a chill stealing up her spine. "You know I'm supposed to marry someone back home." She couldn't possibly go through with it, but Trixie didn't know that. God, would Mama ever forgive her?

"But is that person a prince?"

She hesitated. "No, he's the son of a baron."

Trixie waved her off. "The prince outranks him. Therefore, forget him." Then she narrowed her lavender eyes at her. "Unless you love this fiancé."

"Heavens no!" She gasped. "I'd rather die an old maid."

Trixie tilted her head.

Sighing, Clara explained. "This man is not of my choosing. My parents chose him for me."

"Then you should introduce them to Prince Klaus."

"If only..." She stared off through the window at the setting red sun. It was too bad Klaus hadn't gotten to her papa first. If all Mama cared about was money, Klaus would certainly be her first choice. But how would that work with him coming from another realm?

She sighed. Tomorrow was her first battle as a trainee mage. She hoped and prayed they would be victorious.

"I'd better go. Thanks again, Trixie."

"Have a wonderful time, Miss Clara!" Trixie curtsied and fluttered her wings, which Clara had insisted she leave out in her presence. Staff were prohibited from flight, but she liked Trixie just the way she was and didn't want her to feel uncomfortable. Frankly, she envied Trixie's wings and could never keep them hidden had she been born a pixie.

Klaus stood at the bottom of the crimson-carpeted staircase, waiting for her. He'd shed his military jacket in favor of a hunter green coat with matching cravat, a gold brocade vest and white pants. As always, his boots shone.

"Afraid I'd get lost?" She looked up at him from beneath her lashes, inwardly thrilled to see him again.

"More like afraid someone else would capture your attention." He lifted her hand to his lips and pressed a kiss to her knuckles.

"How are preparations?" She hooked her hand around his elbow as they made their way towards the banquet hall.

"Coming along nicely. Did Mother Gingerbread explain the plan to the mages?"

"Thoroughly."

"Are you nervous?" His azure gaze searched hers.

"I imagine anyone would be."

"We have thrown you to the wolves, as Uncle Ludwig says. I can't say how sorry I am that it turned out this way."

"That's not your fault." Clara spoke firmly. It was the Mouse King that had spread his reign of dark magic, instead of taking care of his own people. If he'd been happy with what he'd had, they wouldn't be rushing to train a new mage.

Of course, that would mean that Klaus would have never gone back for her. She would have lived her entire life without knowing the truth of what happened that night ten years ago. So, she was grateful to the Mouse King for bringing them back together.

Almost.

The ballroom's doors stood wide open, with a whirlwind of activity inside. If only her mother could see this. Dwarves, pixies, mages, and men in soldier's dress roamed the huge, circular room. A chandelier of magic orbs of all colors hovered in the center of the ceiling. And scarlet drapes lined the two-story arched windows encircling them.

Klaus insisted she sit next to him at the head table, pulling out the chair next to his. "I've not seen you all day, and I should like to enjoy your company."

"As you wish, Klaus," Clara responded, secretly pleased.

Galiena sat to his right in the center of the head table, with his father and Mother Gingerbread. When the chair on her left slid back, Clara had to look twice.

"My dear goddaughter, I trust everything is going well?"

"Godfather!" His left eye, the one he always covered with a patch, was bare. And it was violet, just as the Sugar Plum Fairy had told her! Her mouth hung open as she gawked.

Ludwig Drosselmeyer slid into his seat, his quirky mouth in a lopsided smile. "Surprised?"

"I'm stunned. Why didn't you ever say anything about this place?"

He lifted a glass of water and hummed. "If I'd known you'd inherit her powers, I would have. But as much as you deserved to know your heritage, I was afraid of you telling your family about it. She made me promise not to tell her husband or her son; she worried others might persecute them."

"Who?"

"Your grandmother."

Clara's brow wrinkled. "But she's been gone a long time." She'd never even met her father's mother; she'd died when he was still a child.

"Yes, so sad. Without access to our Healers, she couldn't survive consumption. And she refused to go home."

"Home?"

Klaus was leaning around her, listening intently to Godfather Drosselmeyer. "Uncle, what are you saying?"

Ludwig sighed and nodded to the servant who lay down their first course. "Children, let me tell you a story."

Chapter 9

Drosselmeyer's story

Blue skies and birdsong greeted Ludwig on the other side of the portal. Spring had come to the Realm of Waking. In the woods surrounding their usual destination, he held the portal open until Marie stepped through.

"Thank you, Ludwig." She smiled at him, his heart beating fast.

"Of course, dear friend."

His pocket watch tucked safely away, Ludwig gallantly held an arm out for her, but Marie ignored it. Friends. That was all she'd ever let them be. He'd be smart to remember that. Her blonde hair seemed to glisten brighter in the strange yellow sun than it ever did back home.

Marie carried a basket of fruit on her arm, dressed in a gown that he'd tinkered to mimic the current fashions of the Realm of Waking. Together, they walked to the market in the square. Bringing her here went against the previous

Sugar Plum Fairy's orders of leaving the veil closed. But his niece-in-law had just ascended to the throne, and there was no explicit law against portal travel. Only revealing themselves and the Realm of Dreams would get him into actual trouble.

Every week Marie shed her identity as the preeminent Caster, set to take over as head mage, to don the identity of a mysterious fruit seller. She'd arrive in the Realm of Waking with rare delicacies she'd only barter. Which had led to her infatuation with a certain human.

Gunther Stahlbaum.

A member of the Realm of Waking's minor nobility, Stahlbaum had made a name for himself as a merchant which led to his title granted by the leader of this region. Ludwig believed the man's name to be Kaiser, but he couldn't be certain. He didn't pay attention to this realm like Marie did.

Speaking of the devil....

"Good morning, sweet Marie."

"Gunther!"

Every week Ludwig wondered to himself why he continued enabling her. And every week, he remembered why when she saw Gunther. Somehow, the man made her glow like a star.

"Ludwig, how are you?"

"I'm well, and yourself?" Her story painting them as siblings had wrenched a knife in his heart. The man in front of him did not know they were in fact competing for Marie's love.

Ludwig knew who the winner was. He just hadn't accepted it yet.

She had explained away his eyepatch as the result of a bandit attack that had killed their parents. Which, as her "only surviving relative," forced him to chaperone the two lovebirds on their weekly date. He'd watched the other man court the woman he loved for far too long.

And today it came to a head.

"Ludwig, might I speak to you in private?"

He nodded, moving into the next room of the house where Gunther entertained them regularly. Gunther slid the study door shut.

"I would like to ask you for your sister's hand in marriage."

Ludwig's blood turned to ice. He blinked rapidly, the need to keep up the illusion of merchants from this realm clawing at his love for Marie. She couldn't stay here! Her magic would die. And he... he didn't know what he'd do without her. Did she love him? No. But he *needed* her.

Sensing his conflict, Gunther tried to persuade him. "I know she's all you have left, but Ludwig, I'm desperately in love with Marie. She will want for nothing. And you would always be welcome at our house."

A tendon in his neck twitched, and Ludwig tried to stretch it out without Gunther noticing. "I need time."

Gunther nodded. "Of course."

Ludwig stepped past him to the door of the study, then turned around. "You will love and cherish her always?"

"Until my dying breath."

He pursed his lips, unable to give an answer yet. This was something he'd have to discuss with Marie. According to their own customs Gunther didn't need permission, like he would had he been courting a human woman. "We will return next week. I shall give you my answer, then."

Gunther nodded as Ludwig opened the door.

"Marie, it's time to go."

Bewilderment at his curt announcement colored her face, but true to their act, she followed him without question. She bid her suitor goodbye, and they strode down the cobblestone street. He had to force himself to let her catch up, grimacing when she clutched his sleeve to keep from tripping.

"Ludwig, are you well?"

"I can't discuss it here."

She blinked her big brown eyes up at him, her confusion clear. It would be so easy to just tell Gunther no. To leave her ignorant of the human's intentions. He could take back the trinket she wore to keep her human form instead of a doll's, trapping her in the Realm of Dreams.

Their failure to return would be answer enough.

But he was also Marie's best friend. So, Ludwig knew by keeping her to himself, he'd shatter her trust in him, and destroy the only relationship she would give him.

What choice did he have?

"She was so excited, so in love with your grandfather. I helped her disappear. And I went to visit every Christmas; it was easier to only cross over once a year. After her death, I continued to check on the family. That's how your father came to know me." Sadness hung over Godfather Drosselmeyer's head like a veil. Even without him saying so, Clara felt the love he'd had for her grandmother. So much love he'd let her go.

"I sent a letter to your parents before I left the realm. They should have it by now. I told them I took you traveling with me."

"They won't be happy about that. They'll think I'm shirking my duty." She shook her head, stuffing down her feelings of guilt. She'd deal with her parents later. "There's still one thing I don't understand."

"What's that, child?"

"How are you Klaus's uncle, yet you knew my grandmother?"

Drosselmeyer chuckled. "That's easy. I'm actually his great-uncle."

"Oh." She felt silly for having asked, but now it was out there.

Her godfather took her hand in his. "When I say you look like your mother, I mean Marie. You are the spitting image of her." He smiled wistfully. "I should have known you'd inherited her magic."

"Father didn't inherit it because it's stronger in women."

Godfather Drosselmeyer nodded. "It was possible, as I, of course, knew, but I watched for the signs and Friedrich was not a mage. I can't tell you how relieved I was; explaining everything to Gunther would have been dreadful. Especially once Marie was gone. It was bad enough explaining I wasn't actually her brother."

"What did you tell him?"

Drosselmeyer shrugged. "That I was a family friend, and she was an only child. That in order to take care of her, I had assumed the mantle of brother so no one would question it." He gave her a sad smile. "Not that far from the truth."

She threw her arms around his neck. "I'm so sorry you lost her."

"I am only sorry she missed out on her legacy." He patted her back. "She would be so proud of you." She released him, and he leaned forward. "Marie would be head mage, not Zelda Gingerbread, had she stayed here."

She gawked. "That's quite a statement."

"It's true."

"Those are big shoes to fill, Godfather."

He smiled at her, his violet eye twinkling as he winked. "And I think you shall surpass her."

Throughout dinner, Clara reflected on her godfather's story. Pieces kept falling into place, drawing an arrow to point her towards the Realm of Dreams. That's why he'd always called her a Dreamer. Why she'd associated them with him.

More and more, she felt like she belonged here in this realm more than her own. Could she really follow in her grandmother's footsteps and abandon one world for another?

Klaus did his best to distract her from her thoughts when the dancing started. She laughed and twirled in his arms. Here, all was right with the world. They could address her worries later; for now, she wanted to cherish this time with her Nutcracker Prince.

After the banquet and dancing, Klaus escorted a glowing Clara back up the stairs to her wing. She'd turned plenty of heads, but she'd only had eyes for him. And no one would dare approach her when it was clear who her date was.

Sometimes it was good to be the prince.

Uncle Ludwig's revelation had stunned him. The prince's heart soared when he realized she was a Dreamer by birth. She *had* to be permitted to stay in the realm!

But the reason for the celebration weighed heavily on his conscience. It was a sendoff, a last night of merriment before the soldiers and mages set out to do battle with the mice. To say he was conflicted would be an understatement. On one hand, he had the utmost faith in her and to hear she was the granddaughter of such a prestigious mage gave him hope for the coming fight. However, the danger she'd be in was no simple thing to accept.

As they ascended the steps, Klaus laid his hand over Clara's. "Promise me you'll stick close to me tomorrow."

Her mood sobered immediately. "But the other mages —"

"Please." He stopped and turned, taking both her hands in his. "I will never forgive myself if anything happens to you."

She squeezed his hands; her face was serious. "I can shield you, too, you know."

Klaus nodded. "You can. And I would be grateful for it." Her eyes widened, and he grinned. He'd surprised his Caster. "But I won't be able to focus if I'm wondering where you are."

"Will you be able to focus if I'm nearby?"

"I certainly hope so." He leaned forward and kissed her soft cheek. At her hitched breath, he pulled back and started walking again. There were still people lingering around the entrance to the castle, and he wanted to keep her to himself while he could.

She seemed deep in thought as they continued to the guest suite doors.

"Klaus, you brought me here so I could fight, right?"

He stilled. He hadn't realized it, but yes, in his desperation, he'd brought her here to do exactly what they were doing tomorrow.

She continued without him answering. "Did you change your mind?"

"No... not exactly." She meant so much to him now, and seeing her in the flesh differed completely from clinging to a memory. "Do you regret coming with me?" Uncle Ludwig would take her back in a heartbeat.

"Never." Clara turned to him, her mouth set in a line. "But if you hold me back, then it was all for nothing."

"I would never hold you back." Klaus was going to kick his own ass for letting her think that. "Even as a child, I saw how fierce and brave you were. And you're going to be amazing tomorrow. I'm just..." Worried. No, terrified something would take her from him. Whether that was a mouse's sword or an engagement back in the Realm of Waking, Klaus was running scared.

Because he loved her.

Her eyes softened. "I know." Klaus's heart stuttered as she reached up and cupped her hand around his face. "But I need you to trust me."

"I do." That got him a smile.

"We'd better rest for tomorrow."

Klaus pressed his hand over hers and laid a kiss on the inside of her wrist. She shivered.

"Cold?" She shook her head, but he smiled. "Let me warm you up." He pulled her hands around his neck and wrapped his arms around her. Pressed breasts to chest, he took her plump lips and kissed her like a man coming home from war.

Angling his head this way and that, he tasted every inch of her mouth. This new realization made him desperate for her. He didn't dare say anything yet; Goddess forbid he distracted her from their task tomorrow. There would be time for confessions when they returned home. When her knees went slack, it set off an alarm in Klaus's brain — he needed to stop this now before he did something Clara might regret in the morning. Pulling back, he took in her flushed cheeks and the glazed look in her eyes.

"Klaus..."

"I'm keeping you from your rest, lovely. You should go." He held her waist steady as she got her legs back under her. If he carried her to her bedroom, he knew he'd never leave. When she pressed another goodnight kiss to his mouth, he held perfectly still.

"Good night, My Prince."

"Good night, my Clara."

It wasn't until she closed the door that he realized she hadn't corrected him.

Chapter 10

"Miss Clara, time to get up!" The sound of Trixie's voice roused her from a dream; a nightmare with her and Klaus surrounded by mice while her parents' New Year's party went on around them. Shaking her head, Clara opened her eyes to see an inky sky scattered with stars peeking through the curtain.

Throwing off her covers, she hurried to the bathroom. When she returned from her morning routine, Trixie had laid her mage robes out on the bed. They were a cinch to throw on once Trixie laced her stays. A quick spell from Trixie and her hair braided itself and wrapped around her head, out of the way. Clara sat on the bed while Trixie laced up her Caster boots. A mage's uniform warded off other magic, as well as bullets, but a direct hit, or a close melee battle, could still injure her.

She pushed the thought down deep. Fear had no place today.

The mages gathered in the stables. A pixie servant pressed a breakfast pastry into her hands while she waited her turn to be assigned a horse. Two of the mages she'd trained with yesterday sat in a supply wagon while stable hands hitched up a pair of pale draft horses. When it was her turn, she wanted to leap for joy when she saw her horse.

"Tinsel! You're alright." The brown mare nuzzled her outstretched hand, then checked her for crumbs. At the stable hand's confused look, she said, "Last I saw her, we had quite the adventure."

He cleared his throat. "They're waiting up front, Miss."

"Thank you." Her robes were no hindrance in mounting this time, and she gently guided Tinsel to wait with the other mages.

"Clara!" Mother Gingerbread's horse trotted over to her. "You're with me."

"Yes, Head Mage." She guided Tinsel to follow the other horse up towards the front of the line. There, astride his stallion, Peppermint, was Klaus.

He looked dashing in his red and gold uniform, the one he'd worn in their first impromptu battle together. Mother Gingerbread rode her horse up to his right-hand side, and he waved Clara up to his left.

"How are you this morning?" he asked with a brilliant smile.

Her stomach rolled, and she hoped that her breakfast would not make a repeat appearance. She swallowed hard. "Nervous."

"You'll do fine," Mage Gingerbread called across. "We're ambushing them. A piece of cake."

Thank goodness her trainer had faith in her. Clara gnawed on her lower lip. What if she couldn't keep up? She'd never forgive herself if she had to go home with her tail between her legs. Had Klaus done the right thing by bringing her here for this war?

Klaus leaned over to whisper in her ear. "I have every faith in you as well." Their eyes locked over the short distance between their horses. He licked his lips, and she swore he was going to kiss her in front of the entire army.

Her cheeks flushed with heat at the thought.

As if realizing where they were, Klaus pulled back, regret in his eyes. But he reached over and squeezed her hand. She squeezed back, that slight gesture saying so much.

The sun had barely risen when Klaus gave the order to march. Clara hadn't seen this part of the country on their brief tour. The road from the castle eventually turned to dirt instead of the gingerbread cobblestone, and the trees grew thicker as they went along.

Despite the sun beating down in the lavender sky, the forest shielded them from sight. After riding half the day, the general from the front line rode back to Klaus.

"Your Highness, we have reached the caves."

"Wonderful. We will rest and refuel here before we continue on."

Clara sat with the other mages when lunch came around. She pushed herself to eat; her appetite was nowhere to be found. While she chewed on some thick bread, the other mages whispered around her.

Someone shoved a mage named Brandy in front of her. "Hey!"

"Go on, ask her."

"Why don't *you* ask?"

"Because *I* won the game!"

Clara's brow wrinkled in confusion. "What game?"

"Nothing." Brandy waved her off. She had dark hair braided around her head, just like Clara's blonde ones. Trixie called them "battle braids." They kept the Caster's hair out of their faces when fighting.

"What's going on between you and Prince Klaus?"

She fought to keep the blush from her cheeks, but she wasn't sure she succeeded when the snickers started. "We met ten years ago. His uncle is a friend to my parents."

"So how come you didn't train with the rest of us?" Brandy asked with a sneer.

She chewed slowly, unsure how to handle Brandy's attitude. When she'd swallowed, she decided the truth was the best option. "I was born in the Realm of Waking."

Then the voices surrounded her.

"That's not possible! What *really* happened?"

"Stupid story for a *late bloomer*."

"Only *Dreamers* have magic."

She couldn't bear to look up in the face of their criticism. The air was thick, and her throat tried to close. What had she been thinking, trying to fight alongside these women? They had far more experience, and hadn't had to rush their training like she had. She was a farce, an imposter.

Thankfully, Mother Gingerbread came to her rescue.

"Knock it off! The enemy is out there." She pointed through the caves. "Not here. We have an ambush to win."

"Yes, Head Mage." The Casters sang in unison. Grumbling, they returned to their meals. But not before Clara overheard someone scoff, "Prince's pet."

Mage Gingerbread glared, and the whispers ceased. Then she sat herself down next to Clara.

"I'm sorry. You don't deserve that."

She shrugged, her whole being numb. "It's not your fault."

Zelda shook her head. "They should know better than to question my judgment."

"They seem more concerned with my relationship with the prince."

Rubbing the bridge of her nose, the head mage leaned in to whisper. "That's because he hasn't chosen a princess yet."

"What?"

"A bride. Whoever the prince marries will be Sugar Plum Fairy after Galiena's time is over. Traditionally, when there is no female heir, the prince marries a mage. Galiena has made no secret of the fact she wants him to choose someone soon. They think they're in competition for the prince's hand." She smirked. "But there's no contest. You captured his heart ten years ago."

Her heart pounded in her ears and her voice came out in a higher pitch. "You remember me?"

"Of course. I was there for the celebration. You captivated him, even as a boy."

Lunch forgotten, Clara sank into deep thought. If Klaus chose her to be his princess, would those mages finally accept her?

Her whole life, she'd run to books to escape her life. Fairy tales with princes and dragons. And in her mind, every prince had looked like her Nutcracker.

She'd eschewed courtships prior to the Berengar fiasco. Perhaps that's why Papa had decided without her. But the more she thought about it, the more she realized that she'd fallen for Klaus as a teenager. Could it be fate like he said?

Clara loved the way he treated her, the way he deferred to her, and the way he held her. She wasn't just safe with him; he *heard* her. He cared for his people and listened to them as well.

And she... she cared for him.

No, she *loved* him.

But now was not the time to dwell on it; she didn't dare distract him. After the battle, after they returned home victorious, she would tell him.

For a moment, she daydreamed about staying in the Land of Sweets and marrying Klaus. Could she lead his people? Surely he would help her. They could be a true team, like her parents were.

"I wish you could stay." She wished the same.

When lunch was over, the mages were the first group to enter the caves. It would take them until evening to reach the other side, then they would ambush the enemy camp when night fell. Clara tried not to think of the sweet mother she'd met in the storeroom. Hopefully, her mate wasn't here.

She'd rather just attack the Mouse King instead of going through his minions. But she wasn't in charge.

True to his word, Klaus kept her with him. He marched in the back of the mage contingent, just in front of the artillery. Only the cannons had kept their horses, the guns too heavy for the soldiers to pull. She ignored the whispers and dirty looks from her fellow Casters. They were just jealous. She'd prove herself in this battle and then they would stop.

Mother Gingerbread led the way through the dark, dank tunnel. She was glad for Klaus's grounding presence. Eventually, they had to strike a few torches to see; Zelda had ordered the Casters to save their energy for the battle ahead, so their magical lights were out of the question.

In the darkness, Klaus grasped her hand. "Don't forget your promise, Clara."

"I'll do my best. But I'm expected to stay with the other mages," she whispered back to him.

Torchlight flickered over his face as he begged her with his eyes. "Mage Gingerbread knows what I asked of you."

"She knows more than that." Clara swallowed, and focused her gaze dead ahead. "The Casters don't like me. They called me your pet."

His hand squeezed hers in a vise. "Does it bother you?"

"Yes," She blurted out, her volume still low. "I want them to take me seriously."

He heaved a sigh and released her. "I'm sorry. I'm not sure if I should help or if that would make it worse."

"It would be worse, I'm sure." She reached for his hand once more. "But you're forgiven."

She could stand any embarrassment as long as he stood by her.

"You'll show them today. I have faith in you. Then they won't bother you anymore."

"It's hard. I feel so at home here, but most of the people must see me as an outsider."

He squeezed her hand again, reassuring her, but said nothing.

The closer they got to the end of the cave, the quieter everyone became. Even the horses seemed to understand the danger. When they found the end of the tunnel, Mage Gingerbread called for a halt with a hand gesture.

Ahead, all she could see was a stone wall. Then the wall glowed as their head mage chanted. When the spell was complete, the wall disappeared, and the tunnel opened to the Land of Flowers.

The sun must have set while they traveled; now it lay low in the sky, its reddish glow highlighting the strange flowers that grew along the hills.

"Wow." Clara barely breathed. She wished she could see it in the light of day; the colors looked exquisite.

Klaus strode to the front with his captains and Mage Gingerbread, bringing Clara with him. Someone pulled out a map so they could determine which direction the mouse camp lay, and they set off.

Mage Gingerbread led the mages in, casting a huge silence shield, to muffle the sounds of their march. She had trained with the other Casters on this just yesterday. What surprised her was that they could cast it on people and not just a room.

The army smothered their torches as they moved out. The tunnels had let them out only a mile or so from the camp, whose fires glowed in pinpricks in the darkening night. Two of the mages went with the artillerymen, and the rest clustered on the hill above the camp.

Clara frowned down at the silent group of tents and campfires. It was dinnertime, yet the camp was utterly silent. Not a single mouse moved between the tents.

She tugged at Klaus's sleeve and whispered into his ear. "Where is everyone?"

Concern marred his features in the flickering light. Then his eyes widened in fear as the hairs on the back of her neck lifted.

A voice cried out in a strangled gurgle from the back of the group.

"We're surrounded!"

Chapter 11

Klaus choked on the gun smoke from dozens of rifles, both the enemy's and their own.

"Push them back!" he cried, and pulled Clara behind him as he drew his sword. Red lights lit up the night as the Casters began their attack.

"Klaus, I need to go!"

"Stay close to Mother Gingerbread."

Horses whinnied and reared, as their guides tried to turn the guns around to face the enemy. A cry of "Cut them loose!" rose from the artillery general.

Klaus let the lieutenants do their job until he spied the mouse captain. There, in the scarlet light from the Caster's missiles, stood the sword-wielding mouse in the white headdress from the Enchanted Forest. He crossed his arms over his chest, watching his gunmen fire on the Sugar Plum army.

Klaus stiffened. He'd gotten the best of him before, but now Klaus had an *army* behind him.

Creeping up behind his riflemen, Klaus waited for the volleys to end. Men fell on both sides. Then Klaus rushed into the line. He bared his teeth, then launched himself at the captain, taking him by surprise. Their swords clanging, he pushed the mouse back from his men with an iron fist. Cutlass met saber once more. His enemy backed up ever further, and Klaus herded him towards the lines. Let the men get a shot at him.

Unfortunately, in his rage, Klaus didn't consider that the mouse soldiers might risk their captain's life.

Fire bit into his arms and across his side. He staggered back, and a scream erupted from the Süssland side. A white light engulfed him as red magic pummeled the mouse army.

Then the world went black.

A cool breeze wafted across his cheek. The mattress under his back was hard, but the pillow was soft and warm.

"Thank you, Annika." A familiar voice, choked with tears.

"My pleasure." Fabric rustled and footsteps carried someone away.

Quiet murmurs surrounded him, but gentle fingers threaded through his hair, and he nearly fell asleep. But before he could, he remembered.

The empty camp. The battle. The mouse captain.

Clara!

His eyes snapped open to find her staring down at him, a white orb of light hovering nearby, haloing her in a glow. "Clara," he groaned and tried to rise, but his side burned. He gasped at the pain and laid back down. She'd pillowed his head in her lap.

"Klaus!" Warm salt water dripped off her chin and down onto his face, where she brushed it away. "Sorry. So sorry."

"Hush. It's alright. I'm okay."

"Annika said it'll take time for you to finish healing." She bit her lip, and he sighed, wishing he could kiss her.

"Did you get hurt? What happened?"

"Nothing serious. Mother Gingerbread called a retreat."

"What?" That brought him upright with a groan. Pain be damned. "Why would she do that?"

"They'd overtaken the artillery. We had to destroy the guns to keep the mice from turning them on us. At that point, I was still shielding you and I —"

"Wait. That was you?"

She nodded, her voice trembling. "I — I was so scared."

Clara had saved him yet again. Klaus shuffled closer so he could cup her head in his hands and thumb her tears away. "You're amazing."

"Your Highness!" Zelda Gingerbread approached them, her purple robes marred with smoke and mud. "You're awake."

He refused to take his eyes off Clara. "I am."

"Remind me not to make your girl mad."

The girl in question blushed and turned away. Klaus cocked his head at Mother Gingerbread, not questioning that she'd referred to Clara as his girl. "And why is that?"

Zelda put her hands on her hips and stared down at them. "When you got hit, she not only cast a shield around you, but she started pelting the enemy with missiles faster than I've ever seen. It takes a special mage to cast two spells at one time, and she was casting dozens simultaneously." The elder mage shook her head. "I don't understand how she's a Waker."

"She's not." At her confusion, he continued. "She was born there, but Uncle Ludwig knew her grandmother, who was a Dreamer."

"Her grandmother?"

Clara nodded, then lifted her head to the head mage. "He said she was a Caster named Marie."

"Well, no wonder!" Zelda threw her hands up in the air. "Wait, Marie Zuckerman died ages ago. How are you her granddaughter when she was never even married?"

"She left the realm and married a human named Stahlbaum. My grandfather."

Mage Gingerbread chuckled. "I'll be. You know, when I saw you in your battle braids, I thought you *were* Marie for a second. But I figured I was just going senile."

Klaus laughed despite the stabbing in his ribs. Zelda Gingerbread would never lose her faculties. She was too stubborn.

"It's time for a debrief, Your Highness. And then we had better get back."

"What of the tunnel?"

"It's closed off again. They won't be able to break that enchantment once we're done reinforcing it."

"Good." He struggled to his feet, clenching his jaw at the sear of pain through his side. The Healers' magic had fixed his more superficial wounds, but that rib shot would haunt him all day.

He took one last look at Clara. "Thank you, yet again, for saving me."

"Anytime," she whispered, then rose to her feet. "I'll see if there's anything I can do to help. See you when we ride out."

"Of course." He'd make sure of it, now.

He strode after Mother Gingerbread on her way to where the lieutenants were convening, and his chest tightened. All around him lay the sobering effects of the battle. Healers hovered over soldiers and mages alike, while the few uninjured, or the ones that weren't too bad off, carried provisions to the rest. His people were smeared with dirt and blood.

Klaus's steps grew heavy as the fatigue caught up on him. His first battle as leader and they'd been forced to retreat from what was supposed to be an ambush. He should have called the whole thing off when he realized no one was in the camp. The army of the Land of Sweets was in disarray. He had failed them.

The lieutenants saluted when he arrived, and he returned it, almost grudgingly. They had to be judging him for the way he tried to take down the mouse captain by himself.

"Glad to see you back on your feet, Your Highness."

"Thank you, gentlemen. Your report, if you please."

Lieutenant Braun began. "Unfortunately, we lost fifty percent of our company."

Bile rose in the back of his throat. "Fifty?"

Mother Gingerbread tried to comfort him. "That includes injuries, Highness. And the mages are all accounted for."

Klaus was afraid to ask his next question, but it had to be done. "How many soldiers are dead?"

"Twenty percent."

He released the breath he hadn't realized he was holding and closed his eyes. "The enemy?"

"They suffered many casualties at the mage's hands, but we're not sure of the number."

He'd led his first battle, and he'd failed miserably. "It's no matter, they were only a small portion of the mouse army."

"As were we, Highness," Lieutenant Braun assured him.

Lieutenant Sauer spoke up for the first time, his voice grim. "It was a draw, and that's being kind."

Klaus resigned himself to the loss. Being so close to the tunnel wasn't helping his stress any. "How soon until we move out?"

"As soon as we load the injured soldiers onto the wagon, and double up riders on the horses. Marching back this soon is going to be difficult."

"Leave no one behind."

"Yes, My Prince." Lieutenants Sauer and Braun saluted him once more, and after returning it, he turned to Mother Gingerbread.

"Head Mage, a word?"

They stepped towards the edge of the space their company occupied. "What do you think of Clara?"

"She's got a lot of power, but it needs refining. And it seems to mostly spike with her emotions." Zelda shook her head. "We don't have much time. The Mouse King *will* strike back."

"I know." Klaus clenched his fists in frustration. "I put her in needless danger just to save us."

"She's one of us by blood, Klaus. I don't think you made a mistake here."

He sighed, but nodded anyway. "I appreciate you saying so. But without time to refine her power, how are we supposed to win?"

Zelda shrugged. "There are... ways to enhance a mage's power."

"Like Uncle Ludwig?"

The head mage started fidgeting. "I don't think a Tinkerer's charm is going to be enough here. Talk to Galiena, she may have an idea."

Klaus narrowed his eyes. Mother Gingerbread was hiding something from him. She knew, but didn't want to say. "I'll do that, thank you."

She bowed her head and returned to her mages.

He wandered through the makeshift camp, helping to lift the wounded as he passed through. Despite the chill, dark forest, and the grim defeat, all Klaus felt when he spied Clara was the racing of his pulse. She had reunited with Tinsel, who nuzzled her face and nickered at her.

"I'm glad you're okay, too, Tinsel."

"Clara?"

She startled and turned to face him. "Yes?"

"We have to double up on horses to get everyone home. Are you comfortable with someone else riding with you, or would you rather ride with me?"

His love bit her plump lip, then answered. "I can help carry someone." He swallowed hard with a nod of acknowledgment.

Gingersnaps. He wanted her riding on Peppermint with him, but she wouldn't turn away from someone in need.

Damn, he loved that about her.

Yes, after fighting his feelings for several days, Klaus had to admit to himself that he was in love with Clara. He had been since that fateful Christmas Eve ten years ago.

She was staying in the castle. There would be time for a private conversation later. And plenty of kisses for his savior.

Klaus resigned himself to riding by her side again. They both hosted a wounded soldier with them on their mounts. The artilleryman assigned to Klaus had taken some serious hits. His black coat hid the blood, but the dirt showed he'd given the mice as good as he'd gotten.

"Thank you, Your Highness." Before Klaus could even ask his name, the man slumped over Peppermint's neck, dead asleep. He leaned forward and patted a startled Peppermint.

"It's alright, boy. Our friend here has had a very rough day."

He swiveled to see Clara assisting a young soldier into Tinsel's saddle behind her. The young man's arm dangled in a sling and he sported a bruised eye that would certainly be purple by the time they arrived. "Can you hold on?" She asked the man with concern in her voice.

"Yes, ma'am." He wrapped his one good arm around Clara's waist. "The name is Felix."

She turned her sunshine smile onto Felix. "Nice to meet you, Felix. I'm Clara."

Klaus's chest burned as he ground his teeth. When Felix's eyes grew wide, Klaus realized he was glaring. But he wasn't sorry.

As it turned out, Felix had a girlfriend. When Clara asked about her, he'd waxed poetic for most of the ride home. He made it very clear after only a few minutes he had no designs on his girl.

Good.

A somber company entered Sugar Plum Palace as dawn broke. Even the horses' heads drooped. His failure churned in his gut. And he still had to face his parents and explain what went wrong.

Had their intelligence been faulty? Or were the mice just that much smarter than them?

Silent villagers greeted them in the palace courtyard. Parents sought their children, afraid to call out in case they weren't among the survivors. Klaus's heart broke further. He'd failed them as well. How could he face his people?

He helped the injured artilleryman off Peppermint. The poor man had dozed the entire ride home. Two of the Healers swept him away and half-carried him towards the infirmary.

Clara eased down off Tinsel, handing her reins to a stable hand. "Take good care of her for me, please."

"Yes, Miss Mage."

As the young boy led the mare away, Klaus gave in to the urge to reach for her. "I need to meet with my parents, but could I see you afterwards?" he asked as he led her towards the palace.

"If I'm not asleep, Your Highness."

"None of that. You're not my subject."

She cocked her head at him and crossed her arms. "Am I a Dreamer, or not?"

Gingersnaps, he really put his foot in his mouth this time. "You are, but I would have you call me by name."

"As you wish, Klaus." She spoke low. "I didn't want them to think I was getting special treatment."

Some of her hair had escaped her battle braids, and he tucked it behind her ear. "But you are special."

"Klaus..." That word held a warning. Too many people around them for this.

"I will come to you after I speak with my parents. And wash up." He was sure he stank.

That got him a chuckle. "An excellent idea. I'll be waiting." She winked and strode away, up the staircase to the guest suite.

Leaving him to make his way to the war room. He recalled Mage Gingerbread mentioning ways to amplify Clara's power. He would ask his mother about it and hope that his parents would trust him to fix this.

When he knocked at the sturdy wooden door, he heard his mother call, "Enter." Galiena and Alaric sat in their dressing gowns, clearly having just awoken when they arrived.

"Mother, Father, I... The battle didn't go as I expected."

Father's brow furrowed in concern. "What happened, Klaus?"

"We lost twenty percent of the soldiers, and both artillery guns had to be abandoned." At their astonished looks, he continued. "They were waiting for us." He explained what he knew of the battle, and that he'd nearly had the mouse captain. "The lieutenants assured me we did some damage to their numbers, but with Mage Gingerbread calling for a retreat, it's hard to say."

"This is most concerning. Alaric, did someone compromise our network?" The Sugar Plum Fairy asked while pursing her lips.

"It's always possible, my love. I have not heard from the spy network since our last meeting. They could have captured someone."

"Clara saved us," Klaus told them. "Mother Gingerbread said she cast dozens of spells simultaneously, allowing us to retreat."

And saving his skin, not that he'd admit that to his mother *again*.

"Dozens? That's impossible."

"She said her power needs refining, but we don't have a lot of time. But she mentioned there's a way to enhance a mage's power and told me to ask you about it."

Galiena considered it. "A Tinkerer's charm? I'm sure Ludwig would make her one."

Klaus shook his head. "No, she said there was something stronger."

Understanding dawned on his mother's face. "Well, there is one, and it would work for any mage."

He had to know! "What is it?"

The Sugar Plum Fairy huffed. "Last time I brought it up, you weren't thrilled with me."

"What are you talking about? We've never discussed this."

She chuckled. "My dear son, if you, as the Prince of the Land of Sweets and Toys, marry a mage, her powers will become ridiculously strong. It's a result of the land accepting a new potential Sugar Plum Fairy. I've been trying to get you to take a bride for years."

Klaus blinked at her. Was it really that easy?

"I want to marry Clara."

Galiena sputtered. "Where is this coming from?"

Her words drifted past as he floated on the air, all his concerns removed. "This is perfect. She's the strongest mage we have. Just ask Zelda. And she's a Dreamer by blood."

"Yes, Ludwig informed us." Father crossed his arms and sat back. "Son, are you sure?"

"I've never been more sure of anything in my life." At his mother's skeptical look, he continued. "Ten years ago, before she left the realm, we kissed under the mistletoe."

"You were just a child then!"

"It doesn't matter. The mistletoe has spoken, and... I've known for a long time no one else will do."

"*That's* why you went back." She glanced at his father and her expression softened. "Ask her quickly. If she agrees, we'll have the wedding tomorrow." Mother sat back down in her chair. "Klaus, I did not know."

He ran a hand through his hair, then winced when he pulled a twig out of it. "After everything that happened that night, I didn't want you to be even angrier with me."

"Son," Galiena was up and out of her chair, opening her arms for a hug. "A match blessed by the Goddess? I never would have been angry."

"Well, I didn't know she was a Dreamer by blood, either."

"True."

Father also rose and grasped him in a hug. "The mistletoe is never wrong." He threw an arm around Mother. "It showed us the way."

Klaus grinned. "I'm going to clean up and then go see her."

"Good luck, son."

Chapter 12

F reshly bathed and dressed in another gown, Clara paced the guest suite sitting room. Klaus had yet to make an appearance. She should sleep, but her mind wouldn't let her. Trixie had taken her mage robes to be laundered, so she couldn't send a message with her. Huffing, she sat down at a small desk in the corner.

On a hunch, she lifted the lid and found a pen, ink, and paper. Perfect. Dipping the pen in the ink, she etched out a quick note.

Klaus,

I'll be in the courtyard.

Yours,

Clara

Folding it into thirds, she wrote his name on the outside and left it tucked between the French doors to the suite as she left. She took her time descending the stairs, her skirts rustling. The palace was abuzz, people scurrying about.

She meandered toward the courtyard door that Klaus had shown her their first day here. Goodness, had it really only been two days? She'd lived a lifetime in this realm. If she returned to her own realm now, she'd never survive. The magic buzzed within her, and she loved it. Every day it strengthened; going home would mean smothering it forever.

She could no sooner do that than cut off her arm.

The sun shone pink in the lavender sky. Would she miss the blue sky of her own realm? Godfather Drosselmeyer would surely take her back to visit if she did. But how would she explain to her parents that she wanted to stay in this realm and break their engagement plans for her?

Trixie's suggestion that she trade Klaus for Berengar rang in her ears. She absolutely would, in a heartbeat.

Klaus caught up with her as she wandered toward the arbor they'd kissed under her first night back. "Clara!"

She spun to greet him. "You got my note."

He nodded. "How are you not exhausted?"

"I couldn't possibly sleep after that battle."

Taking his arm, they sat on a bench in the sun, free of mistletoe distractions. Clara welcomed its warmth. Klaus had cleaned up post-fight, donning a casual shirt and vest.

"I'm sorry I took so long. There was something I had to find."

"It's alright. I just couldn't sit still any longer."

"Magic usually takes energy out of a mage."

"I rested when you were unconscious." Her cheeks warmed, remembering how intimate it had been to cradle his head in her lap.

He leaned in and whispered, "Next time my head is on your thigh, I want to be awake to enjoy it."

She gasped at the impropriety, even as she laughed. "You're a terrible tease."

"Only for you, my darling." His gaze caressed her face. "I love you."

Her vision went hazy until there was only her, Klaus, and the bench they occupied. "Klaus..."

"If you really want to... marry your fiancé, I'll make sure you get home. I won't come between you. But —"

"No!"

Klaus's face fell. "N-no?"

Oh no, he'd misunderstood. Clara shook her head. "Klaus, I can't *stand* Berengar. He's my brother's best friend, and the two have lived to torment me my whole life. I plan to tell my parents I can't go through with it as soon as I get home."

He smiled and slid closer, wrapping an arm around her and pressing their foreheads together. "It's your life and your future, not theirs. Don't do what your family demands, do what *you* want."

But she wasn't finished. "Besides, how can I marry someone else when I'm in love with you?"

Klaus pulled back to look at her face then. "Praise Asteria..." he murmured, then pressed his lips to hers. She melted into him under the heat of the sun, bringing the fires only he inspired to life under her breast. Any feelings of guilt she had left burned away. All too soon, he released her, but before the fires could cool, he slipped off the bench and laid one knee in the grass.

"Clara, my love, you've saved my life multiple times now. It's yours. In fact, I've been yours since that first battle ten years ago." Klaus dug in his pocket, then held out a gold ring set with a ruby-colored gem in a shaky hand. "Will you make me the happiest man in both realms, my love? Will you marry me?"

"Yes!" Her breath came in quick gasps, tears of joy falling down her cheeks as he slid the ring on her finger. This. This is what she wanted, more than anything, she thought to herself as Klaus picked her up and spun her around.

She'd gotten everything she'd ever dreamed of — magic, freedom, and the love of her Nutcracker Prince.

Klaus held her fast and spoke in her ear. "How do you feel about a really brief engagement?"

"How brief?" Clara pressed her damp cheeks against his shirt.

"Mother says your magic will get even stronger when we wed. It's part of the ceremony."

She could hardly believe she was considering it. "But the mouse army..."

"It's up to you. Mother can arrange for the ceremony to happen tomorrow here at the palace." Klaus looked down into her eyes. "In our Realm, a woman's parents have no say in who she marries. She decides for herself." He hesitated, then continued, "I'm loathe to take you back without tying you to me. Part of me is worried that swine will come for you."

Clara shuddered. He had a good point. The best way to ensure she didn't have to marry Berengar was to marry someone else. She wanted to stay here, anyway. As Klaus's bride, she could have everything she wanted.

"I don't know if I'm worthy to be the next Sugar Plum Fairy."

"Mother will train you, and I can help you when we get to that point. Provided the Mouse King doesn't have his way."

She clung to him then. "We won't let that happen."

"See?" Clara heard the smile in his voice. "You're already talking like a queen."

"Don't weddings take time? And what will the people say about us getting married at a time like this?"

"It will thrill the people to have something to celebrate. And with magic, it takes no time at all." He released her. "Unless you're not sure. I don't want you to feel pressured."

"I'm sure." She loved him. In fact, she was pretty sure she'd fallen for him at thirteen. No wonder she'd been drawn to her books. No human man could ever compare.

"Can we visit my parents, like Godfather Drosselmeyer?"

"Of course." He kissed her palm, and her pulse jumped. "I won't ever keep you from them."

She bit her lip. Were they worried about her? What would they think if they knew the truth of what happened, instead of the tale her godfather told them?

It wasn't unusual for a relative to take a young adult traveling with them. For companionship and help. But to do so without warning was odd.

Her grandmother, Marie, had been in the same position all those years ago. And she found the strength to disappear from her realm so completely they thought her dead. All for the love of her grandfather.

Clara's heart swelled with light. Staying in the Realm of Dreams would bring her grandmother's legacy full-circle.

"Tomorrow, you said?"

Klaus shifted on his feet. "Mother might have told Cook to be ready to bake the wedding cake."

Nervous giggles erupted out of her like champagne bubbles. "Let's do it then."

He let out a whoop and spun her around again. "We better go find Mother, my beautiful bride."

Klaus raced through the palace, Clara by his side. His cheeks hurt from smiling. Servants dodged out of the way with knowing looks on their faces.

"Klaus! Slow down!" She called through her laughter. He did as she asked when they reached the foyer. Oh dear. His bride was out of breath.

His bride. How wonderful that sounded.

When she nodded, they continued up the stairs that led to the family wing, albeit at a slower pace. "Do you want to see our rooms first? Where you'll live with me?"

A sweet cherry blush came over her cheeks. "Maybe after we talk to your parents."

"As you wish." He kissed her knuckles and led her to his parents' suite at the back of the hall. Knocking on the tall double doors, Klaus fought the urge to bounce on his toes.

Father was the one to open the door. "Come in," he said with a smile on his face.

Clara pressed close to him, curtsying to Galiena.

She tsked. "None of that in private. We're to be family, yes?"

His fiancée rose and nodded. Mother opened her arms and hugged Clara tight. "Thank you for making my son happy."

Clara hugged her back, and he saw tears forming in her eyes again.

Father hugged her as well. "When do you want the wedding, you two?"

"Tomorrow, as Mother suggested."

"If it's not too much trouble, Your Majesty," Clara added.

"Please, call me Galiena. Or Mother." She took his fiancée by the arm and led her to the couch. "I believe we have much to discuss for tomorrow. I shall call for Cook and the royal Tinkerer so we can get everything prepared." She waved Klaus off when he tried to sit next to them. "This is girl time. I believe your father has something he wants to discuss with you."

His brow furrowed. He looked at Clara. She gave him a smile and a nod. "It's fine, Klaus. I'll be right here."

"I wanted to give her a tour of the family suite."

"You shall. After tomorrow." His mother gave him a sly grin. "After all, you should have a wing to yourself for your wedding night." She turned back to Clara. "If the guest suite suits you for it, that is."

"That would be fine."

"Come, son. I have to talk to you." Alaric led him out of his parents' sitting room and down the hall. Klaus opened the door to his own rooms, sensing his father wanted some privacy for this discussion.

He hated to leave his betrothed so soon after proposing, but they had a lot to plan and not much time to do it.

Alaric went to the bar cart Klaus never touched and poured himself a shot of liquor.

"Father?"

He looked back at Klaus. "You may want some for this discussion. Although I will start by mentioning that I had to have it with my father-in-law, which was supremely uncomfortable. So perhaps not." Father poured a second shot, anyway. "We need to talk about your wedding night."

Klaus laughed. "Father, we discussed this ages ago when I was a boy. I know what to do."

Alaric sighed and drank his alcohol. "That's not all you need to be aware of. Especially when you're counting on Clara's magic increasing."

Now he was getting self-conscious. "What do you mean?"

"Her magic doesn't actually increase because of the ceremony. It starts there, yes, but it increases with the wedding night specifically."

Klaus strode over and took the glass off the cart, then downed it. "So consummation is required?"

"To release her full potential as the Sugar Plum Fairy, yes."

He shook his head. "I can't imagine having this conversation with Grandfather."

Alaric shuddered. "It was awful. But I digress." He poured a second shot and knocked it back. "How much do you know about pleasuring a woman?"

Klaus just blinked at him. Nothing. He knew absolutely nothing. With Clara out of reach, he'd never so much as *seen* a naked woman.

"I was afraid of that. Settle in, son, it's going to be an interesting afternoon."

Chapter 13

The next day flew by in a blur of activity. Clara was pampered and scrubbed within an inch of her life. Royal Tinkerers used their magic to prepare an exquisite white lace wedding gown fit for a princess. Trixie ensured she ate, shooing other servants away to give her space to breathe.

"This is madness," she muttered to herself over lunch.

"Madness?" Trixie tittered. "The kingdom is buzzing with excitement." She flew around the room, expressing her own. "You've given us hope, Clara. That's more than we've had since the mice invaded the Land of Flowers."

Clara furrowed her brows. "It feels like such poor timing, to be so happy when we're at war."

"Do you need a torch in the daylight?"

She huffed a laugh. "No, of course not. It would be a waste when the sun's shining."

"Exactly." Trixie crossed her arms over her chest. "We need this now, like we need a torch in the nighttime."

Their exchanges were so similar to her conversations with Heidi that she felt a pang of homesickness. Rubbing a hand over her chest, she hoped Heidi would be alright when she didn't return. Her friends would wonder what happened to her…

"Trixie, how long do I have before I need to get ready?"

"About an hour, Miss Clara. What do you need?"

She popped the last gumdrop into her mouth and rose. "I'm going to write a couple of letters to mail when I visit the Realm of Waking. I don't know how they'll write back… I'll ask Godfather if it's possible."

In her heart, Clara knew hearing of her marriage to a prince of a faraway land would thrill her friends. Perhaps Adelia or Francesca could hire Heidi away from Mama and Papa if they were so inclined. She wished things were different, but she couldn't bring her dear maid to the Realm of Dreams.

Writing to them would help fill her time before she became Clara von Süssland.

A knock at the door drew her attention away from Trixie's spell for her hair. "Who is it?"

"It's Galiena."

"Goodness!" Clara nearly ran Trixie over on her way to the sitting room. "Come in!"

Galiena swept into the room in a ruby red, long-sleeved gown. "My dear, you look exquisite." She held a wooden box in her hands.

"Your Majesty? I mean, Galiena?" She shook her head as she corrected herself. That would take some getting used to.

The Sugar Plum Fairy merely smiled. "I wondered if you would do me the honor of wearing this today." She lifted the lid of the box to reveal a gold tiara studded with crystals.

Clara gasped. "It's beautiful."

Galiena smiled. "It's our tradition for the princess to wear this on her wedding day, and for court days thereafter, until her coronation."

She gulped as the sunlight sparked rainbows off the headpiece, throwing them to the wall and carpet. "The honor is all mine."

Her soon-to-be mother-in-law slid the tiara into place in the intricate up-do that Trixie had done. Then she turned her to face the mirror on the wall. Clara's mouth fell open. She really looked like a princess!

"Thank you, Galiena." She fought back the tears.

The Sugar Plum Fairy herself gave her a watery smile and a gentle kiss to the forehead. "Welcome to the family, my dear."

Another knock at the door. "Clara, are you ready?"

"Godfather!"

"She still needs her veil!" Trixie sniffed, her voice teary, and flew into the bedroom to retrieve it.

"Well, look at you. Friedrich's going to be so angry with me when he finds out about this." Ludwig grinned despite his words.

"If it weren't so urgent, I'd have told Klaus I wanted to bring my parents." Clara bit her lip, starting to second-guess herself. "But I really don't want to wait." It would take too much precious time to explain everything to her parents, and then there was the fact they were a realm at war. As upset as she'd been over their promise to the von Galens, she didn't want them in danger.

"You let me worry about that. I can handle your papa." He patted her hand as Trixie flew over her head, laying a long, sheer, white veil over her head. The lace on the edge of the floor-length veil matched the trim of her gown. Crystals, like sugar on gumdrops, sparkled in the light among the lace design.

She couldn't wait for Klaus to see her.

"Just let me pin this in place," the blue pixie said, sticking her tongue out as she eased the hairpin to hold it down. "I'll find you after the ceremony and help you take it off."

"Thank you, all of you." Clara fought back tears.

"No crying until we're all seated, young lady." Godfather Drosselmeyer wagged his finger as he teased her. He'd shed his usual attire for a formal black silk coat and trousers. "I don't want to lose my composure in front of the entire kingdom."

Her throat threatened to close on her. "The... the *entire* kingdom?"

"Ludwig!" Galiena smacked his shoulder. "You'll scare the poor girl."

Clara breathed in and out slowly. She could do this. She'd better get used to the whole kingdom having an interest in her. After all, that was part of marrying Klaus.

And he was waiting.

"Let's not keep Klaus waiting."

Galiena smiled. "I'll see you down there."

Godfather Drosselmeyer led her down the stairs and through the hallways to the courtyard. That was where the couple had chosen for their ceremony, under the arbor with the mistletoe. They felt it would be a good omen, and honor the Goddess he'd spoken of.

"So should I call you uncle after this?" she teased.

"Godfather is still fine. I'll answer to pretty much anything except 'late for dinner.'"

She giggled, then sobered. The door to the courtyard was coming closer.

"I'm doing the right thing, aren't I?"

"Do you feel you are?"

"I can't imagine marrying anyone else. I just hate to lose my parents, too."

Ludwig shook his head. "You won't lose them. I can take you and Klaus back every Christmas Eve with me."

"Promise?"

"I swear to you."

A few steps closer. "You loved my grandmother."

"I did."

"Why didn't you tell her?"

"She didn't feel that way about me, and I knew it. But it doesn't matter. Everything worked out the way Fate intended." Ludwig patted her hand. "I wouldn't want to live in a world where my great-nephew doesn't have his Clara."

She took a deep breath, pushing tears back once more. Her godfather understood what she was giving up best of all. Because he'd helped Marie do the same. "I hope I'm an acceptable replacement."

"Of course, child. Now," he said as he put his hand on the door. "No crying yet. At least let an old man sit down before he makes a fool of himself."

She grinned at her silly godfather. Then he opened the door and led her outside.

The music changed. Citizens of the Land of Sweets and Toys stood as she entered the courtyard. Clara floated down a crimson aisle runner on Drosselmeyer's arm from the door to their archway. When she caught sight of Klaus, everything else fell away. He stood at the end waiting for her next to their dwarven officiant, in a white coat with gold epaulets and buttons, his boots polished to a perfect shine. A small gold crown shone atop his head. His eyes and smile glittered in the sunlight. All for her.

"You look beautiful," he whispered on a breath when he lifted her veil. Then they stood, hands clasped, before the priest.

She couldn't recall exactly what he said, or what vows he had them repeat. There were some additional promises made as the future rulers of the land. Part of her wondered if that was part of the ritual to enhance her powers. But mostly she marveled that this was happening at all.

"You may now kiss the bride!"

Cheers erupted from the gathered crowd of citizens and servants alike as Klaus bent her body back and kissed her with intense passion. She clutched his neck until he raised her once more. The band played the recessional, and they walked arm in arm back toward the palace.

"Are you alright?"

"You kissed me silly!" Her head still spun a little. He laughed, then leaned in close so only she could hear.

"Just wait until tonight."

Well, she certainly fit the blushing bride stereotype *now*.

Their receiving line took forever, as the wedding was open to the entire Land of Sweets. Clara was grateful when someone ushered her and Klaus into the ballroom. Once they sat down, the party began.

She waited throughout dinner, but nothing felt different. After she and Klaus cut the fabulous cake that Cook had made for them, there was still no change. Where was this increase in her magic?

Before the dancing started, she tapped her new mother-in-law on the shoulder. "Galiena, could I speak with you for a moment?"

"Of course, dear." She patted Alaric on the hand and turned to her. "What is it?"

"Klaus said my magic would increase, but I don't feel any different."

Galiena's cheeks turned a pale shade of pink. "Well, it doesn't actually come from the ceremony."

"It doesn't?"

"The ceremony is still necessary, to open the door, if you will." Goodness. She hadn't seen the queen so flustered before. "The power surges with the consummation the night after."

Gingersnaps.

Klaus approached the two most important women in his life, grateful to the Goddess they were getting along. He reached for his beautiful bride. "Come, it's time to open the dance floor."

She slipped her hand in his, but her smile didn't quite reach her eyes.

"Darling, what's troubling you?"

"It's nothing."

They swept into the area cleared for dancing. He wrapped his arm around her back and drew her into the waltz as the band played. "I don't care if it's the tiniest thing, anything that upsets you is never 'nothing,' but especially today."

She worried her lower lip, which only made Klaus's concern grow.

"Do you not like dancing?"

"No, that's not it! I've been looking forward to this all day."

"What then, my love?" If she were having second thoughts, he'd release her from the marriage, no question.

"I'm just worried."

He pressed their foreheads together, and her eyes fluttered shut. "Please tell me. I don't want secrets between us."

She pressed a gentle kiss to his mouth. "I will, but not here."

Klaus nodded.

As the song ended, he realized other couples joined them on the dance floor. He and Clara were lost in their own realm, somewhere between dreaming and waking. Klaus couldn't believe that mere days ago, she'd had no idea he was real. And now they were married.

They danced the night away, and his bride seemed to relax as the reception went on. At her first yawn, however, he decided they had stayed long enough.

"Shall we slip away?"

Clara nodded, that blush coming over her cheeks again. She tucked her hand in his arm and he nodded at his father to let him know they were leaving.

The silence rang in his ears as soon as they left the ballroom. He hadn't realized how loud the reception was until he was away from it.

His bride clung to his arm, and he realized she was trembling. "Darling, what's wrong?"

"Not here."

She hurried him up the stairs. When they arrived at the guest suite where Klaus's parents had advised them to stay, he had to block her from opening the door.

"Can I carry you over the threshold?"

"Is that a tradition here too?"

He nodded. "Please, I don't want to risk any bad luck tonight. It's been so perfect."

"Then you may." She wrapped her arms around his neck, and he turned the knob behind his back, then bent to lift her into his hold.

"Look at me." Clara lifted her doe eyes to him. He could see the fear still inside, and he did not know what to do about it. "I love you."

"I love you, too."

He backed into the room slowly, then turned and kicked the door shut. She made to jump down, but he held firm. "I'm not putting you down until I get to the bedroom." She was rushing him, and he wanted to savor every moment.

Thankfully, the door was open, so Klaus had no trouble getting inside. He placed Clara on the bed, then slanted his mouth over hers. Perhaps kissing her silly again would help.

When he pulled away, she had that dazed look in her eyes. Gathering her hands in his, Klaus kneeled on the floor. "Now, what's upset my bride, and who do I have to kill?"

That made her giggle. "You've no malice in your voice. You won't kill anyone tonight."

He grinned. "That all depends on what you say next."

Clara sighed.

"Please, tell me what's wrong."

"I'm just scared."

"Scared of me?"

"No..."

"That sounds more like a yes, my love." Klaus broke out in a cold sweat. "I swear I would never hurt you."

"I know you wouldn't do that on purpose. It's just..." She looked away. "Your mother said that in order for my magic to grow, we have to... um..."

He raised his eyebrows. "Consummate?"

"Yes, that." Her cheeks flushed cherry red. "And *my* mother told me the first time hurts, and I'm just nervous, that's all."

What was wrong with these human men? Did they not know how to pleasure their women? The discussion with his father had been awkward, but he'd left Klaus with a book or two to study while the women made wedding plans.

He licked his lips and stroked Clara's arms to calm her tremors. "I can't say I've any practice, but I swear to you if anything I do hurts, tell me and I'll stop."

"But we have to —"

"We don't have to do anything you don't want to. Magic or not, I won't hurt you."

She huffed out a breath, and her hands clenched into fists. "But the whole point of coming back for me was to defeat the Mouse King, and without more magic, we'll lose!"

Her voice had taken on a note of panic, and Klaus shook his head. Gods, this was all his fault. "Darling, I used that as an excuse. I had to see you again. I should have come for you *years* ago, but I was a coward. Invasion or not, I would still want to marry you. Please forgive me for ever letting you think otherwise."

Her breasts rose and fell as her breathing became rapid.

He couldn't wait any longer to taste her lips again. Sliding onto the mattress, he hauled her into his lap and let his tongue speak for him. She moaned and gripped his jacket, popping her mouth off his and gazing up at him with hooded eyes.

"Klaus... take this gown off."

Chapter 14

"**A**re you sure?"

Clara couldn't possibly *not* want him after that beautiful speech. The ache between her thighs began again, and she needed him to fix it. To fill her. "I trust you." She waited a beat before adding, "Husband."

He cupped her cheek and searched her gaze. "That is a high compliment indeed. Wife."

She grinned. For so many years, she'd dreaded this day that she would lose her freedom, but she'd never been happier. "You unwrap your wedding present, and then I'll unwrap mine."

"Ladies first, My Princess." Klaus dropped on to his arms and leaned back on his hands.

Clara let her hands roam over his handsome coat, fingering the golden buttons, then pushing them through the buttonholes. She caressed his chest and opened the jacket, shocked to find he wore nothing underneath when she pushed it off his shoulders.

"No shirt?"

Klaus shook his head. His firm muscles were the next target for her wandering fingers, while the ache in her loins blazed.

He sighed and closed his eyes. "That feels wonderful."

Clara still had unwrapping to do. She stood, and he watched as she unfastened his pants and slid them down his legs with his drawers. He helped her remove his boots, and only once he was naked did she dare look at him.

"That's... going inside... me?" She squeaked.

"The decision is yours." He stroked his length as he gazed at her. "Now, it's my turn."

Clara swallowed as he stood and kissed her breathless again, his shaft pressing into her stomach. The flesh was hot, or maybe it was her? His lips gently nibbled her ear and down her neck, then he went around to her back and kissed her nape. She shivered.

"Cold, my love?"

"Not at all." Fire burned in her belly.

He unhooked the bodice at the back, and she fought the urge to hold it up. Klaus came back to face her and slowly peeled it down, revealing her corset and chemise. Gently, he lifted the precious gown and laid it on a chair near the bed. He stared at her body for a long moment, then lifted his head and blinked.

"I have no idea how to do this." His hand traced the top of her corset, making the skin of her breasts pebble.

Clara stifled a giggle. "Petticoats next."

With her guidance, Klaus finished undressing her, then looked his fill. His hands hovered over her as if she were a priceless vase.

"Touch me, *please*."

He lifted her into his arms and laid her on the bed. She thought it would combust from her arousal. Then his hands were everywhere, and his lips and tongue followed. When he suckled at her breast, her back lifted off the mattress like she was going to levitate.

"Klaus!"

He just chuckled and rolled her other nipple under his thumb, eventually switching sides. When she whimpered, he let his hand trail down to where she ached.

Her hips jolted when his finger swept through her folds. "You're drenched."

She covered her face with her hands.

"No, no, that's a good thing." He pulled himself up and kissed the backs of her hands. "I'm going to stretch you so it won't hurt, alright?"

Clara lowered her hands to the bed and nodded.

"Relax, my love. It's just me. You can tell me to stop." He hovered over her, watching her face as his finger returned to her core. Slowly, he slipped it inside her.

"Oooh." That felt so good. Like finding a missing piece of herself that she hadn't noticed before. He withdrew all too soon, and she pouted.

"Open up and let me in, darling."

Her legs spread immediately, wanting more of that fullness. Klaus lowered his mouth to hers and his tongue swept inside at the same time his digits did. She kissed him back as his finger withdrew and thrust again and again. She had a fever, and he was the cure.

Her prince. Her husband. Klaus swallowed her moans as her body swallowed his fingers. First one, then two, then three. Her nails dug into his buttocks as she silently pleaded for more.

Then his thumb swept the top of her slit and hit a button she'd never known about before, and she felt the fire within blaze brighter. She broke away from his mouth to moan his name.

"Clara..."

"Do it. Now!"

Hesitation written all over his face, Klaus moved his hips between her legs. But the magic was rising within her, an energy vibrating faster and faster, along with the blaze of heat. The time was now.

Full. So full. Klaus slotted himself slowly inside her core, and her walls convulsed. He bent back down and kissed her again. "*My* Sugar Plum Fairy. *My* queen."

Sliding. Thrusting. Harder. More. Faster. Yes. Yes. *Yes!*

A white light with the strength of the sun eclipsed them as they both cried out.

Klaus snuggled Clara deeper, her blonde hair spread across their pillows. After the explosive magic-enhancing climax, he'd taken her twice again last night, at her urging. He'd been afraid she'd be sore, but she said the magic eased any pain.

He was the luckiest Dreamer in their history.

She nuzzled her bare skin against his, and he sleepily considered taking her again as the morning light pierced their sanctuary. Until he realized what had woken him.

A peppermint horn sounded in the distance. That was the guard sounding the alarm.

Klaus bolted upright, throwing his bride off him.

"Klaus?" She rubbed her eyes.

"Get dressed. Invaders!"

She popped out of bed and they pulled their clothes on. The servants had moved his magically shielded jacket and pants to the guest suite, as well as his sword. He was ready in a flash.

Poor Clara had too many layers. "My stays, quickly!"

"Why bother?"

"You would have me fight *unbound*, husband?"

Klaus considered the implications. While pleasant for him, he'd have to rip out the eyes of every soldier. "I'm coming, love."

He tightened the laces and tied them for her, then she threw her mage robes over her head and slipped into her Caster boots. She brushed out her hair as he belted his scabbard to his waist.

"Klaus... I'm scared."

His stomach churned as he held her close. He'd only just found her! "Let me call Uncle Ludwig to take you home."

"No! I just... I wanted you to know." She buried her face in his shoulder. "No secrets, remember?"

"Right."

Her arms tightened around him. "I chose this. I chose *you*."

His brave, fierce Caster. As much as he wanted to ensure her safety, he couldn't deny her anything, even something dangerous. "I love you." Klaus pressed a kiss to her temple.

"And I love you."

As much as he'd like to stand here and hold her, their kingdom was under attack. "We don't have much time. My parents will be in the war room."

"Let's go."

They ran for the sitting room, where Klaus grabbed her hand. Panicked voices echoed from the hallway. What would they find outside these doors?

Servants and panicked chaos met them in the hall. He held onto Clara, and they bolted to the stairs, jockeying for position among terrified citizens. There was no time to figure out what others were supposed to be doing now. Klaus's mission was to get to the war room.

Guilt swamped him as he witnessed the quiet fear and determination in the eyes of his citizens. This was his fault. He'd failed them in the Land of Flowers and now they would pay the price.

His head down, he let her pull him along the corridor as servants pulled tapestries down from the wall, rolling them up for safekeeping. Slipping inside the door, Klaus found his mother and father, as well as the spy from earlier, in the war room.

"You!" Anger rose in him, and he jumped ahead of his wife. It was *this* man's fault that the mice had known about their ambush! "The mice thwarted our attack in Blumenland!"

The dwarf, Heinrich, winced. "My apologies, Your Highness. They knew more than I realized."

"We have more pressing matters, son," Galiena chastised him.

"But how can we trust his information?"

"It's corroborated by the information sent by the border guards," Father answered.

Klaus still eyed Heinrich warily.

"I swear by the Goddess Asteria, My Prince, I did not betray my country." The dark-haired dwarf's gaze didn't falter.

Klaus clenched his jaw. Ultimately, blame didn't matter; the enemy had breached the wall. Failure was not an option.

"What do we know?" Clara's voice was timid. Klaus moved back to bring her forward. "What's the plan, Your Majesties?"

Mother gave her a perturbed look, but didn't address the use of their titles. "Defensive maneuvers. The border guards gave it their best, but the mice caught them unawares."

"Where will the people go?"

Klaus wrapped an arm around his princess. "They'll have gone into hiding. With any luck, they can stay there until we address the threat."

"He wants to rule the entire realm." Alaric explained. "He'll be coming straight here."

Clara nodded.

"The guards are watching for the invaders. Once we see them, we'll know which section of the castle they'll be attacking."

"What's the most likely target?" Klaus crossed his arms as he studied the map.

"In all honesty, they're likely to come through the front door. There's only one way in." The Sugar Plum Fairy's mouth set in a firm line, and Klaus knew what his mother was thinking.

One way in, and one way out.

They were trapped.

Chapter 15

C lara had never seen the mages in such disarray. It seemed the call of the horns had pulled everyone from bed, even Mother Gingerbread. While Zelda's short locks meant she didn't need battle braids, most of the mages did. Women lined up to braid each other's hair along the tan ramparts as Zelda led them through a meditation.

She focused on the head mage's words, her newly expanded magic swirling within her. The energy inside felt chaotic, like a new puppy, pulling her to run, jump, and play. But this wasn't playtime.

Her mentor led them through the exercise to sharpen their magical focus. When she blinked her eyes open, everything appeared in sharp relief. White lines surrounded each mage, encasing them all in a glow.

Looking down at her hands, Clara gasped. She glowed the brightest of all. This must be the result of her increased power and the battle meditation. She could literally *see* the magic.

Flutters erupted in her stomach, and she nearly turned down the breakfast breads being passed through the mages. But they had warned her in training that fighting on an empty stomach was a recipe for disaster. Plus, who knew when they would have time to eat their next meal?

A tap on her shoulder had her spinning around. "Princess, are you alright? I've been talking to you, but you didn't answer."

Princess... that was her, right? "S-sorry, it's so loud I couldn't hear you."

"No matter." The mage, whose name escaped her, grinned at her from beneath heavy red bangs. "You didn't join in the braid line?"

"I ... I don't know how to do them yet." Her stomach sank to the gingerbread ramparts below her feet. Here she was, princess and future ruler of a land, and she couldn't even do the most basic battle preparations. But her fellow mage didn't let her wallow for long.

"Mine are done already. Here, let me do yours."

Clara followed her down to the floor and chewed her breakfast while her comrade went to work. She was so used to Trixie doing her braids by magic that having her fellow Caster work on her hair felt... different. Comforting, even.

She prayed Trixie was safe. There hadn't been time to call for her, and from the mess inside, it sounded like even the servants were preoccupied with the battle to come.

She thanked the girl, who still didn't give her name, before the redhead ran off into the chaos. Turning, Clara sought Klaus, who was speaking with his generals, Alaric, and Mother Gingerbread.

As she neared the command group, a cry of impending doom rose from the gathered fighters. Despite the early hour, the skies grew darker, a shadow spreading over them from the south.

"They're coming straight for the front gate, as Mother predicted."

She jumped at Klaus's voice in her ear. "How do you know that?"

He pointed to the darkness spreading across the sky. "The Mouse King's dark mages blot out the light because it can weaken the spells they cast on him. He's coming with the army."

Dread clenched her stomach, and Clara trembled. She'd thought she'd have more time before facing the seven-headed Mouse King. But he was coming.

"Are the villagers safe?"

Klaus shook his head. "As safe as they're going to be."

"We need to take out the bridge."

An explosion rocked them then, and the surrounding soldiers cheered.

"Already taken care of." He gave her a tight smile. "But I like the way you think."

She sighed. "Hopefully that will slow them down."

"I can still call Uncle Ludwig." Blue eyes burned down at her. "I will do anything to ensure your survival."

"And I will never forgive you if you do that." She reached up and pulled his head down to meet her lips, pouring her heart and soul into that one kiss. It didn't matter if she was out of her depth, she still had Klaus. "There is no life without you."

Klaus bit his lip and his gaze grew watery. "As you wish, my love."

As the sky grew darker, the wind blew colder, and the surrounding chaos quieted. In the distance, war drums drilled ever closer, their cadence heralding the mouse army.

White mage robes rustled next to them, and she turned her head. The Sugar Plum Fairy herself stood on the ramparts like a beacon of hope. Soldiers and mages alike turned and bowed.

"Citizens of the Land of Sweets and Toys! Today, the enemy thought to surprise us. That after our feasting and celebrations last night, we would be weak."

"No!" called the people.

"We would be unprepared."

"Never!" they answered back.

"That he could take this land for his own!"

Shouts of disgust radiated through the gathered crowd.

"Now rise and crack him like the Crackatook nut!"

A roar of voices and stomps took over the Süssland forces, Clara absorbing their enthusiasm with glee. Until she heard a return roar from deep inside the darkened village.

"Gingersnaps," Klaus muttered next to her ear.

"What is it?"

"I thought they couldn't live outside the Land of Ice and Snow."

"Who?" She looked at her husband. His face was ashen.

He pointed in the far distance, the waning light difficult to make out the shapes. "See those tall, lumbering creatures?"

Squinting into the distance, Clara could see them as the mouse army drew nearer. "What are they?"

"Yeti."

The three yeti were twenty or thirty feet tall, covered head to toe in long white fur, with fearsome claws and fangs. Dull red eyes shone in the dim light, and a spiked metal collar sat around their necks. As the army drew closer to the shore, she could see each had two mice sitting on their shoulders, whips in hand.

A strange trumpeting sound drew Klaus's attention. "No!"

"What now?" She turned to follow his gaze. "What in Heaven's name..."

Two enormous creatures, not quite like the elephants in Papa's books, moved toward the castle. Every step of their flat feet sent tremors through the structure. Covered in white fur like the yeti, they had two icy tusks that curved around in front of their long trunks, which dragged towards the ground.

"Ice mammoths. They're using both to raise siege towers!" Klaus was right. He started shouting orders. "Bring down the mammoths and the yeti! Don't let them raise the towers!"

She ran to join the other mages and pass along the information. Together, dozens and dozens of fiery magic missiles flew over the wall. The beasts continued on, unphased. But her enhanced senses told her something else needed to be done.

Focusing with all of her might, Clara watched as the mouse on one of the yeti's shoulders whipped him when the mages' missiles hit the beast. The collar buzzed with energy. An eerie glow radiated from the collars on the yeti, and matching rings adorned the mammoths' tusks...

"Aim for the collars!" she called out. At the very least, shooting the mice off the yeti would render it directionless.

The yeti all roared, trying to block the shots with the siege towers in their hands. The wooden ladders split in two and fell to the ground, crushing the unfortunate mice who could not dodge. As more came forward, the mages' shots hit their targets.

All three collars shattered, and the dull eyes of the yeti regained their pupils. Shaking their heads as if waking up from a nap, the three creatures looked around in bewilderment. Then the mice on their shoulders did something idiotic.

Their whips cracked frantically, as if that was what had held the monsters under their control. All three yeti swiped the pests off like dust from a jacket and unleashed their anger on the mice below! Clara could hardly believe she'd done that.

Now the mice had a second target, much more mobile than the palace. Another roar to her right made her look over just in time to see the mammoths break free from their captors and a cheer go up from Klaus and the soldiers. Their trunks, outfitted with painful spikes, slammed through the mice at their feet even as the ones on their backs tried to regain control. Those siege towers had to be abandoned too far away to do the mouse army any good.

"Great thinking, Princess!" Mother Gingerbread gave her a look of approval. "Fire on the mice!"

As Clara and the rest of the mages focused all their spells on the soldiers, moans of pain broke her concentration.

The yeti and mammoths were on the ground. Dead by their captor's orders.

More soldiers swarmed forward, and then she realized they had gathered the broken siege towers together to take the place of the bridge.

"No!"

Her missiles came faster from this endless energy well that Klaus had opened in her, trying her damnedest to break the bridge before they could cross it. But a shield of dark magic formed over the mice on their makeshift bridge, protecting it from her assault. Where were their mages? She saw no one that could cast this.

Cannons blasted across the ramparts, but the dark shield held. A cluster of mice at the back of it hurried through the lines toward the path they'd formed across the moat, and then she saw what they carried.

A battering ram, in the shape of one of the Mouse King's terrifying heads.

Klaus grabbed onto the wall as the palace shook. What in the Goddess's name was *that*?

"They have a ram!" cried someone closer to the front.

Well, that answered that question. He peeked over the ramparts to see the mice had fashioned a bridge out of their destroyed siege towers and were now banging on the door.

"Keep firing! Reduce their numbers!"

Bent over to keep his balance, Klaus made his way to the soldiers who were on standby atop the entrance to the courtyard. "Get that syrup ready!" They saluted him with their thick heatproof gloves as they stirred the cauldron of hot, sticky syrup over the fire.

The peppermint canes of the portcullis were thick, but they soon gave way to the iron in the battering ram. So did the beautiful cinnamon wood door that lay behind it. His heart lurched as the enemy breached his home.

The cannons roared their discontent behind him into the mouse army. Squeaks erupted from the mice below, the ram pulled back, and then they descended.

He held his arm aloft as they moved the cauldron into position. When the mice crossed the doorway, he lowered it and the soldiers dumped hot, sticky, boiling syrup all over the first wave of mice. Their screams drowned out the noise of battle until they went silent.

But Klaus knew that would only buy him a few precious moments. He drew his sword and raised it high. "For Süssland!"

The mages and the soldiers split their attentions, but the second wave of mice was undeterred by the syrup that had boiled their countrymen alive.

Clara. He had to get to Clara before the mice overran them.

Soldiers affixed bayonets for close combat and led the way down the stairs to meet the enemy. Crimson missiles of magic whizzed past his head, and the thick scent of gunpowder filled his nostrils. Where was his wife?

Dozens of missiles flew from one corner of the courtyard, and when the smoke cleared, there stood his Clara. Zelda Gingerbread was holding a shield around them while Clara focused on offense. In the center of the courtyard, he glimpsed his parents fighting back to back.

Attackers came from all sides, the grotesque mouse teeth much too close for Klaus's comfort. His saber clashed against their bayonets, beating them back amidst the uncomfortable squeaking language of the mice. Chest heaving, Klaus stabbed one after another, trying to make their deaths quick so he could move onto the next. Sweat poured into his eyes.

The mice backed away from him, surrounding him with their bayonets. He slashed away. He was a prince of the realm and he would not back down!

Then pain erupted across the back of his head, and stars flashed across his vision before it went black.

Chapter 16

M age Gingerbread held her shield, but the mice just kept coming.

"There's no end to them!" Exhausted, Clara's energy wavered.

"Take over the shield!"

She flung her shield out in front of them as Zelda drew back and started bombarding the invaders. Maintaining one spell was not as strenuous as the multiple missiles she'd been hurling. Still, she needed to maintain her focus or the enemy's attacks would land.

Their backs to the outer wall, Clara saw two hooded, stooped figures move through the pandemonium of Süssland and Tierland soldiers. One shuffled towards them, the other faced Galiena and Alaric.

"Mages!" Zelda fired on them, but her missiles did nothing. The mages flung nets of black rope, one at her and the head mage, and one at the Sugar Plum Fairy. Clara spread her shield thin, too thin, perhaps, to cover their heads, but it was no use. The second the net touched her magic, it absorbed it, and fell on them anyway, rendering their magic moot.

"Where did they get this dark magic?" uttered Mage Gingerbread. "It's in the *rope*."

The net sucked the very life out of Clara, her magic that had once filled and swirled within her silent, unmoving. She was normal, a human once more, just like in the Realm of Waking, with no power. Her jaw hung open as she gasped for breath. How had she ever thought she could go back to *this*?

Quiet reigned over the battlefield. The mouse soldiers must have been waiting for their mages to arrive. Someone pulled the net off her legs, then rough hands grabbed her wrists and held them behind her back. No! Grunting, she tried to fight them, but their hands held fast as more magic-dampening rope chafed her wrists and bound her hands behind her.

"Get up, mage," sneered a voice.

More hands lifted under her arms and set her on her feet. Her nails dug into her palms as she fought to school her expression and keep her hands from trembling. She clenched her jaw as she glared at the mouse soldiers lifting her and Zelda to their feet, startling when she saw the mouse mage.

Cloudy, unseeing eyes gazed out from beneath the white hood. Scraggly gray fur covered his (her?) mouse head topped with ragged ears. The swishing tail behind them ended in a blunt cut, instead of the tapered tail mice usually had. Looking over at the second and third mage that joined them, they had the same disabilities.

"To the dungeons with you!" That creepy voice belonged to the mouse mage!

The mages shoved at her and Zelda, herding them into the palace. Galiena and Alaric marched beside them.

Clara's gaze darted around, taking in their surroundings. She was with the two most powerful mages in the land, and they were being pushed into their own castle. Surely, they could get away from some *blind mice*.

They weren't even touching them. Silently, she slipped behind a pillar. The mage whirled on her and glared at her with his white, dead-eyed gaze. "You can't escape, little Caster." She remained motionless. He cocked his head at her, looking at her but not quite facing her somehow. "I *see* you," he hissed.

"Let's move!" Another mage snapped. Her legs began to move without her consent.

"Feisty," said the third. "The compulsion spell will do the trick."

Compulsion spell? No wonder.

Galiena and Zelda hadn't resisted. They must have already been under one or anticipated the possibility.

Clara gave in and let them lead her down the stairs at the back of the castle into the dungeons. She hadn't even known the palace *had* a dungeon! It didn't seem to be built of the same gingerbread as the rest of the building. Instead, the walls appeared lined with iron. Silent soldiers pressed them into a cell, then cut them free. She rubbed at her aching wrists and waited for the magic to return.

The door slammed shut and the four of them were alone. Galiena and Alaric took one bunk along the wall, and Zelda faced them from the other. Clara stayed standing. Still, her powers lay dormant.

"The ropes are gone. Why can't I feel my magic?"

The Sugar Plum Fairy sighed. "We lined the dungeons with spells to dampen it. My predecessors designed them in the event a mage went rogue. That's why the Seers didn't follow us in here."

"The Seers?"

Zelda nodded. "The dark mages that made the Mouse King the demon he is today."

The chilly dampness of the cell crept into her bones. Klaus wasn't with them. A pain made even more apparent when Alaric tucked his wife under his arm.

"Now what?" she asked them.

"Now we wait and see what he wants. The magic of this land will never recognize him, and he knows it. So he'll keep us alive." How could the Sugar Plum Fairy sound so defeated?

"Klaus is out there. He can rescue us!"

Zelda just gave her a pitying look and patted the space next to her. "Take a load off, Princess. You're going to need your rest."

She wasn't sure how long, but some time later, six mouse soldiers appeared in front of their cell. "Come," was all their leader said to them in that squeaky mouse tone. Alaric, Galiena, and Clara were all cuffed with iron that must also dampen magic, and led out of the dungeon. The soldiers forced Zelda to stay behind.

Mice were everywhere. They had pillaged the castle kitchen and never made it past the hallway, laying about and gorging themselves on the palace food. Clara kept her chin steady, as did her parents-in-law.

The soldiers herded them into the throne room. More mice filled the room, not just soldiers this time, but some civilians as well. And there on the dais, laying across the Sugar Plum Fairy's throne, was eight feet of Mouse King.

The seven-headed demon regarded them while leaning on his elbow, his massive tail snaking down the steps to the floor below. His three blind mages stood behind him, their unnerving gazes each looking in a different direction. Yet somehow she knew they were watching their prisoners.

"Well, well, well," the king boomed, and all chatter ceased. His voice differed from the others. No squeaks at all, but it slithered in her ear. She suppressed a shudder. That creature was unnatural.

"If it isn't the Sugar Plum Fairy," he continued. "Or should I say the Sugar Plum *Failure*!" His subjects squeaked at his joke, and Clara clenched her hands at their laughter. He rose to his feet and towered over them. "I am the King of Sweets and Toys now!"

Galiena shook her head. "This land will never recognize you, Ferdinand. Nothing you do can change the magic of this realm."

"Silence!"

But the queen had more to say. "This is not what the Goddess intended —"

"The Goddess?" He hissed from a second head. "The Goddess which granted you magic and not me? *I care not what she thinks!*" A third head roared with the Mouse King's fury.

Then he calmed immediately, as if turning the gas off to a lamp, and the center head spoke once more. "I merely brought you here to return something of yours." With that, a pair of soldiers thrust something into the center of the room. No, not something. Some*body*.

He picked at his nails, already bored. "I'm a father, too. I wouldn't want you to worry about your precious *boy*."

Clara was too busy swallowing around the lump in her throat to shudder at the idea of the Mouse King having kids. She bit back a sob at the sight of Klaus, unconscious and bloody at their feet. Only the soldier's claws grasping her arm held her up.

"What did you do to my son?" Galiena spat.

"He lives. For *now*." The creepy mouse waved one of his paws. "Take them away."

One soldier threw Klaus over his shoulder and they returned the four of them to the dungeon.

Her hollow chest echoed with the knowledge they had failed.

Klaus woke to a gentle hand stroking his face, his head pillowed against familiar thighs. Ignoring the throbbing in his head, he opened one eye to see his beloved. Unlike last time, however, they weren't outside, and he hadn't had a visit from a Healer. His whole body could attest to that. The other eye refused to budge, and he swept a hand cautiously over his face. It was swollen shut.

"You're awake," said Clara.

"I swear we're going to do this someday when I'm conscious."

"Well, you're conscious now, son." Father?

Klaus bolted upright as his mother called out his name. Then he groaned as all the aches and pains hit him at once. He felt like a walking, talking bruise. Torchlight flickered from outside the bars of a cell door, throwing strange shadows through the dungeon. His parents sat on a bunk across from him and Clara.

"Not you, too?"

Galiena nodded solemnly. "Ferdinand has control of the Land of Sweets and Toys."

"Are you alright?" Clara touched him gingerly.

"I've been better." He cupped her tear-streaked face. "You're well?"

"Exhausted, and utterly magic-less. But yes." She leaned into him as tears ran anew. "I was so scared when they brought you out."

He pressed a kiss to her forehead. "They'll have to do better than that to keep me from you." But his words rang hollow. He had failed miserably — again.

Not for the first time, guilt ate at Klaus. If he'd never returned to the Land of Waking, never asked Clara to return and help his people, *their* people... she'd be safe at home with her family.

What had he been thinking? Was this truly what she wanted?

It couldn't be. If he could find Uncle Ludwig, then she could escape.

"Where's Uncle Ludwig?"

"We don't know," Alaric answered. "He could have gone into hiding or they might hold him elsewhere. I don't know if the Mouse King realizes he's a mage."

"I hope he's safe." Clara bit her wobbling lip.

Klaus wrapped his arms around his bride, hiding his wince. He was too tired to keep beating himself up over his past decisions now.

The dark circles under Clara's eyes worried him. With a soft grunt, Klaus stretched back out on the prison bed. "Lay down, my love. You need rest." She didn't argue, just pressed against him on the firm cot.

Wrapping his arms around her, he tried to focus on his memories of their wedding night together. For a few blissful hours, he'd had everything he ever wanted. He offered a prayer as sleep claimed him, that if the Goddess Asteria would find him a way, he'd make sure Clara got to safety. No matter what happened to him.

There was no way to tell the passage of time in that place until the guards brought breakfast. It was little more than stale bread and water, but the prisoners ate it gratefully. The swelling in Klaus's face had gone down, though a spectacular bruise had formed, and he didn't wince as much. Without access to a Healer, Clara and Galiena checked him over for cuts, using some of their precious water to prevent infection. Thankfully, the mice had seemed intent on taking him alive instead of killing him, so he only had the nasty knot at the back of his head where the mice knocked him out, and a couple of incidental cuts on his hands. Her husband wouldn't have survived a stab wound.

The mice had moved Zelda to a different part of the dungeon. Apparently, the Mouse King didn't think it wise to leave the Sugar Plum Fairy and the head mage together, despite its magic-canceling powers.

"Darling…" Klaus took her hand. "If we can get a message to Uncle Ludwig, we should ask him to get you home."

"Klaus, no! I can't leave you."

"It's the safest way."

"Not unless you come with me."

He sighed and ran a hand through his dark hair. "I can't stay in this form on that side of the portal. I'll be a Nutcracker again. And if I disappear, the Mouse King will look for me."

"And you don't think he'd look for me?"

Silenced, Klaus leaned over and pulled her into his arms. His shoulders shook with silent sobs. Clara fought back tears of her own when she looked into his face.

"I just want you safe, love. I'll take whatever he dishes out, but I can't let him hurt you." He stroked her hair, now loose from her braids. "It would rip my heart out to lose you, but I can die content if I know you're safe."

Tears ran tracks through the dirt on their faces. "I'd rather die here than try to live without you, Klaus."

A tearful squeak disrupted their bubble of sorrow. "No dying."

There, at the cell door, was the mouse mother Clara had seen before.

"It's you!"

"Shh!" Miss Mouse put a finger to her snout.

Clara dropped her voice to a whisper. "What are you doing here?"

"I brought lunch." Through a slat in the door, Miss Mouse slid their tray. Bread and water, just like before.

"Where's your baby?" The little one was nowhere to be seen. Had something happened?

"He's with my mate."

Clara smiled. "You have an excellent mate."

Miss Mouse nodded. "You too. Good mates want you safe." She looked to the door of the dungeon, then back at Clara. "I'll come back later." Then she ran off, back to the outside world.

A little piece of Clara sighed in relief knowing the mouse soldier mate was safe. She sat back down, taking the piece of bread Klaus held out to her. "What was that about?"

She felt her cheeks flush. "I saw her outside the castle the day I trained." The lie rolled off her tongue only because they were around the others; she didn't want to say the mouse was in the storeroom. "She was hungry, so I shared some of my lunch. Apparently the mice are all starving while their king wages war. It's terrible." She gulped the dry bread down, then reached for her small cup of water. "She has a little baby and they have nothing." Unable to meet Klaus's eyes, she resolved to tell him the full story later. If they had a later.

Galiena shook her head. "He's so caught up in this idea of ruling the realm that he's forgetting his own people."

"The mice weren't always like this, were they?"

"No, of course not. Ferdinand's father got along with the rest of us just fine. We'd had peace for centuries. But Ferdinand, even at a young age, was obsessed with magic, and jealous of the mages," the Sugar Plum Fairy explained. "His obsession led him to the dark arts, and now it's not only corrupted him, but ruined his own country."

Clara turned to Klaus. "Either way, I'm still not leaving you. We will figure this out."

Her husband sighed. "As you wish."

Chapter 17

At dinner time, Miss Mouse returned with the tray, slotting it in place.

"What's your name?" asked Clara. She'd forgotten to ask before.

Miss Mouse answered her in a series of squeaks.

"Um, I'm not sure I can pronounce that."

The mouse shrugged. "Means 'white flower.'"

"Oh, like a rose? Can I call you Rose?"

Rose nodded.

"You're all dressed up. Are you celebrating something?"

She put her finger to her snout once more, then looked over at the dungeon doors. "There's a big party upstairs for the Mouse King…" Two thumps sounded off at the end of the hall. Then Rose stuck her tail into the lock, using it like a pick until it released. "The guards are out. Let's go."

The door swung open, and the others jumped to their feet. "But Rose, you'll get in trouble! The baby…"

Rose turned her head and spit, just like in the storeroom. "The King put my mate in danger. I won't help him." She pointed at Clara. "You helped me, so I'll help *you*."

"You realize what we have to do, right?" Klaus's voice was cautious, his hands in his pockets.

Tears gathered in Rose's black eyes. "Save us?"

Clara responded immediately. "Of course." Whatever was going on in Tierland had to be awful if killing their king was a blessing.

Her husband was on board. "Where did they put my sword?"

Rose shrugged. "You could take the guards?"

Alaric and Klaus stole the two guards' weapons as they all left the dungeon, the mice snoring on the floor. Hopefully, that would buy them some time.

Galiena spoke up next. "We won't get close to him with those Seers around."

Gingersnaps, she was right. "Where would those nets be?" asked Clara.

"Let's check the armory." Alaric led them down a hall before the door that would take them back out to the main part of the palace. Only two guards for the entire area? That surprised her. Everyone must be at this celebration.

Alaric opened a sturdy wooden and iron door. "Aha!" He wrapped the nets over his arm. "Klaus, I see your saber!"

"Thank the Goddess! I can't figure out how to fight with this cutlass." Klaus hung the mouse's sword up on a hook and took down his own. He slid it into the scabbard at his hip and patted it with a sigh.

Rose watched the door, wringing her tail between her hands. "We need to go! All the mice are in the throne room."

"The throne room?" Galiena and Alaric looked at each other and nodded. "We'll go around the back way."

"What about me?" asked Klaus.

Alaric answered. "You're our distraction."

"What? No!" Clara cried. "They'll kill him."

"The soldiers don't have their weapons at the party," Rose squeaked. "The King doesn't trust most of them."

That was certainly interesting. The King clearly knew he had upset his own people.

"But I need to get back or someone will notice me missing."

After checking for danger, Rose ushered them down the darkened hallway. Alaric and Galiena slipped into the war room as they passed it. "Don't do anything until we contain the mages, Clara." Galiena whispered to her as they disappeared.

Night had fallen, the twin moons shining through the windows. They crept along the wall, keeping to the shadows. Clara stumbled over Rose's tail, who grabbed it in pain.

"I'm so sorry, Rose! Are you okay?"

Rose shuddered. "I know you didn't mean it. It's just, shoes are a mouse's weakness."

"Shoes?" Klaus looked at Clara, and the meaning dawned on them both.

"Yes. They say someone hit our King with a shoe many years ago, and he lost his magic. That's why the Seers ruled in his stead for a long time."

Clara's pulse pounded in her ears. Now she knew what she had to do.

From her tour, the throne room had a balcony up above. That would give her the best chance of hitting her target.

"Klaus, how do I get to the gallery?"

Klaus crouched behind the door to his mother's throne room as Rose, Clara's mouse ally, ran back inside. She was going to grab her mate and baby, so no harm came to them.

He seethed inside to see the destruction at the hands of the mice. Despite knowing their Tinkerers could heal the damage, he hated it had ever come to this. They never should have been able to breach their walls, but the Mouse King had done so. This had to work, or Klaus would consider himself a complete failure.

Taking a deep breath, he raced into the throne room with a roar. "Ferdinand!" The eight-foot demon Mouse King turned on his heel, all seven faces spread in creepy, sharp-toothed grins.

"Prince Klaus!" they all hissed at once. "How did you escape?"

"You *dare* to sit on my mother's throne?"

"It's *mine* now!"

"I challenge you!" An eerie laughing sound slithered from the Mouse King, and the rest of the mice in the room slowly picked it up. But not all. Most of them just looked uncomfortable.

"Very well, Prince. Since my soldiers failed, I shall crush you myself!"

Gingersnaps.

Klaus dodged as the king's mighty tail flew into the air and crashed down to where he had been standing. Drawing his saber, he slashed at it, getting a howl of pain from the king in return. He kept one eye on the back of the dais, where the Seers stood cheering on their monarch.

Between evasive maneuvers and strikes of his sword, Klaus glimpsed Galiena and Alaric entering behind the Seers from the secret passage. Just as they had planned, his parents threw the anti-magic nets over the Seers. The king's roars of frustration as Klaus continued to evade his wrath drowned out their cries for help. Then Alaric slit their throats one by one.

Once the last one was dead, it would all be up to his beloved Clara.

However, his distraction cost him dearly. Goddess, he failed at everything. A giant clawed paw reached out and grabbed him by the throat, raising him up to eye-level with the sneering, grotesque heads of the Mouse King.

"I have you this time, prince! And now you'll never get away!"

"You're... wrong." Klaus scrabbled at the hand holding him hostage.

"Am I?" The terrible face came closer. "Explain."

Gasping for breath, Klaus's vision grew hazy. His heart pounded in his chest. *Come on, Clara. Finish him!*

Clara crawled along the gallery railing, praying the balustrades would hide her from the sight of the mice below. Klaus had skillfully distracted them all, causing a spectacle as he pretended to challenge their enemy.

She sat down behind a pillar and tore off her boot, peeking around it to find the Seers dead in a pool of their own blood. The Mouse King's immense body blocked the sight from the rest of the room. Tearing her eyes away from the gory scene, she choked down the bile that rose in the back of her throat. War was not pretty. She'd do well to remember that as a future ruler.

Clara focused her attention and her magic on the shoe in her hand. She'd only have one chance to get this right. Once the Mouse King knew her plan, it would be useless.

She pushed her energy, her fear, and her anger into the unconventional weapon. Just as Mother Gingerbread had explained that day on the training field, the boot pulsed with energy. But something inside her told her it wouldn't be enough. More, she had to give it more. Then a realization hit her. And she poured in her love for this realm, for the mice that the Mouse King oppressed, and most of all, for her beloved Nutcracker Prince. When she opened her eyes, the soft black boot glowed with pure white light.

She could do this. She could defeat the Mouse King. And once that was done, she'd take her independence from her parents and stay with Klaus.

Clara rose to her feet and turned to face the Mouse King. His focus was on Klaus in his hand. Fear for her beloved spiked in her chest and she roared, "No!" Then she hurled the boot at the Mouse King's seven heads. His concentration broke, and all seven looked at her. It spun through the air, heel over toe, then the magic shoe smacked the demonic Mouse King's main head square in his black nose.

A blood-curdling shriek echoed through the chamber, reverberating off the walls and forcing everyone to cover their ears. The eight-foot monster shuddered and shrank, his crowns falling to the ground in a clanging symphony as the dark magic poured off him. When the mist cleared, nothing remained of the Mouse King but a smoking robe and the seven crowns.

Clara raced down the gallery, to the stairs at the back of the throne room. She leaped down them two at a time and ran across the dais into Klaus's arms. Thank God he was safe! He picked her up and swung her around. But the chattering of the mice surrounding them reminded her they weren't finished yet. She pushed out of Klaus's embrace and raised her hands.

"Mice of Tierland!" Hundreds of beady black eyes turned to her. Rose, in her pretty green dress and carrying her baby, pushed to the front. She dragged a mouse in a soldier's uniform by the hand. Clara breathed a sigh of relief that she'd gotten back to her mate. "We have heard of your king's cruelty. I have seen the oppression of your people, and I know you are not the enemy. You're free now."

Galiena swept up to stand next to her, with Alaric right behind. The mice started their chittering again at the sight of the Sugar Plum Fairy. "I will meet with your ambassador and work out a way for the Land of Sweets and Toys to aid you in recovery." She paused. "But only if your forces pull out of all the other lands."

Squeaks erupted among the mice, and one pushed forward. It was the mouse captain Klaus had fought twice before! He raised his hands, and the voices silenced themselves.

"Send word immediately that all forces are to fall back to Tierland!" Then he approached the dais and took a knee in front of the Sugar Plum Fairy. "Your Majesty, I am Crown Prince Farolf, heir to the throne of Tierland. Please accept my humblest apologies for my role in this tragedy. My father gave me no choice." His head tilted downward. "It's my greatest wish to rebuild what my father has destroyed."

"Rise, Prince Farolf. Let's talk about what your people need and how we can help."

Chapter 18

Klaus slipped his wedding band back into its velvet-lined box and patted it fondly. Clara had requested a bit of acting at her parents' tonight, in order to mitigate their anger. As much as he hated to pretend she was anything less than his wife, he'd do whatever made her happy.

After all, most parents would think that to meet and marry in a week *was* ludicrous.

He slid the formal midnight blue waistcoat over his shoulders and buttoned it, then his coat. Galiena and Alaric were hard at work, taking care of the mess left by the Mouse King, now that the mice had left for their homeland. Aunt Crescentia and Aunt Lorelei were also cleaning up their lands now that the dark cloud had passed.

Soon everything would be back to normal. The soon-to-be King Farolf seemed like a good, sensible mouse. They'd had a long discussion. Apparently, his father hadn't spared him from his oppression. Klaus was looking forward to working with Farolf in the coming years.

Trixie flitted out of his bedroom and bowed in front of him. "She's ready, Your Highness."

"Thank you, Trixie. Have a good night off."

"Have fun, sir!" She giggled and flew out the door in a puff of blue pixie dust.

Clara strode into their sitting room. They had moved all her things into his apartment after the insanity of the past two days. Trixie had styled her hair in the fashion of her home country, and she sparkled in the elegant sapphire silk gown. The snowflake broach at her bosom threw rainbows of light around the room.

"Darling, you look stunning." He leaned in for a kiss.

"Klaus, you'll make us late!" She hummed against his lips.

It wasn't his fault they fell into bed every time he kissed her. They were newlyweds, after all!

She pushed against his chest to break the kiss. "I'm serious!"

"Very well," he sighed dramatically. "Until we get home." Klaus waggled his eyebrows, and his wife blushed.

"You know, it's a tradition to kiss at midnight."

"Then we'll have to leave soon after, I think." Klaus laid her heavy woolen cloak around her shoulders and held it there while she tied it tight.

"I won't argue, my love." She gave him a quick peck on the cheek, then hurried to the door. "To the workshop!"

Uncle Ludwig's workshop had been his refuge during the invasion. A small building on the outskirts of the palace grounds, it was where the Master Tinkerer built his toys and clocks. When they arrived at the small gingerbread outpost, Uncle Ludwig opened the door with a smile.

"Children, you look wonderful!"

"Thank you, Godfather." Clara curtsied, then wrung her hands. "I'm so nervous about going home."

"You leave the explanations to me," said the old mischief-maker, his eyepatch covering his violet eye. He bopped her on the nose fondly. "I hurt my back at Christmas and you couldn't *bear* to let me travel alone, my good, dear goddaughter."

Klaus grinned at his uncle's cleverness. Clara giggled.

"I've finished your gift, my dear nephew." Ludwig held out his hand to reveal a gleaming golden pocket watch. "This is how I remain flesh and blood in the Realm of Waking. You must carry it on you at all times, lest you revert to your Nutcracker form."

"Yes, Uncle." Klaus ran his fingers over the remarkable craftsmanship. The insignia of the Land of Sweets and Toys rose in relief on the cover. And Uncle Ludwig had engraved his initials on the back.

"It's beautiful," murmured Clara.

"Thank you, Uncle Ludwig." He fastened the chain to his vest button and slipped it into his pocket. "I'll treasure it always."

"Alright then. Let's be off!" Ludwig popped his purple top hat on his white hair and cast the portal spell. A brilliant blue light opened into a circle big enough for a man to pass through. Beyond the hole in the fabric of the realms, a wintry evening scene of cobblestone streets and glowing streetlamps greeted them. Klaus stepped through first, then assisted Clara to the other side. Uncle Ludwig brought up the rear, and the portal sealed shut behind them.

She breathed the first air of her home realm in days and tried not to let the lack of magic bother her. It wasn't as bad as when she'd been trapped in the dungeon; no, it still hummed under her skin, but it was quieter now.

Somehow, it had only been a week since she'd last been home, yet she felt as though a lifetime had passed. She was no longer the Clara Stahlbaum her family knew.

The portal had opened behind a garden wall. Godfather Drosselmeyer led them through a stone gate and down to the street. When she stepped onto the lane, she recognized where they were.

Her parents' mansion rose over the hill as they walked up the drive to the estate. Carriages passed them by, the clip-clop of the horse's hooves giving rhythm to the night. The stars came out to twinkle in the evening sky and an orange moon rose behind her childhood home.

"My apologies, my dear. Next time, I shall have the strength to open a portal wide enough for a carriage."

"Well dear Godfather, you certainly should have enough time to recover," Clara assured him. She didn't mind the walk, but she wasn't used to the hills anymore. When they reached the stoop, she took a moment to catch her breath.

Then Godfather Drosselmeyer strode through the front door, which was open wide with all the guests arriving. Clara and Klaus hurried to follow him.

"Good evening, Mister Drosselmeyer — Miss Clara!" Heidi greeted them with a curtsy, then flung herself into Clara's arms when she recognized her.

"Heidi!" Laughing, she hugged her maidservant tightly. She had to wipe tears of joy from her eyes after her friend let her go.

"We've been so worried about you. Where have you been?"

"You wouldn't believe me if I told you, Heidi." Clara took her hands and squeezed them. "But don't let me interrupt your work." The last thing she wanted to do was cause the poor girl any trouble.

Godfather Drosselmeyer put an arm around her shoulders. "She's been traveling with her old, decrepit godfather who hurt his back and needed help."

Her cheeks heated, but she nodded. "We'd better find Mama and Papa before someone else does."

"Come, nephew." Ludwig shuffled into the drawing room, playing up the part of the sore old man.

"Friedrich! Margareta!"

"Godfather Drosselmeyer!" Papa reached them first, Clara hiding behind his form.

"A happy New Year to you, son." The two men shook hands.

Mama came and let him kiss her on the knuckles. When he bowed, she saw Clara at last. Shock came over her mother's face.

"Clara!"

"I've missed you so much, my dear." Papa came forward and hugged her. "Such a good thing you did, helping your godfather in his hour of need."

"I'm only sorry there wasn't time to talk to you about it first, Papa." She let her father engulf her in his warm embrace. Hopefully not for the last time.

Mama stood in front of her and hugged her as well, an awkward encounter as she hadn't been so affectionate since Clara was a small child. "And who is this?" Mama asked, eyeing Klaus.

"Ah yes," Drosselmeyer said with a grin. "Friedrich and Margareta Stahlbaum, may I present my dear great-nephew, Prince Klaus von Süssland."

Klaus bowed to her parents, who paid him equal respect. Mama's eyes were wide when she rose from her curtsy, eyeing him with curiosity.

"A prince, you say?"

"Yes, my brother's grandson." Drosselmeyer smirked at Clara. He knew they had Mama hooked. "Good lad, fine soldier. There's been some issues back home, you see. And Clara has made herself indispensable to Her Majesty."

When Margareta looked at her for clarification, she tripped over her tongue a little. But she got the words out all the same. "Unfortunately, Her Majesty needs me, and that means I won't be able to return for some time."

She looked back and forth between her parents, nerves churning in her stomach.

"Darling, you're too modest. My people hail her as a hero." Klaus gazed at her with unmistakable love and admiration in his eyes. Then he turned to Papa. "I have grown quite fond of your daughter, sir, and I would like to request her hand in marriage."

She hid a smile because, of course, they were already married under his laws.

Papa and Mama looked at each other, communicating silently as they often did. She had never seen them at such a loss for words. Klaus snuck her hand into his arm, and she couldn't help but smile at him. She stood tall with him next to her, loving and supporting her. Hopefully, her parents could see she'd found love all on her own. As much as she knew now she didn't *need* their approval, she found she wanted it all the same.

"But you only met a week ago," stammered Mama.

"Actually, madam, we met ten years ago when Uncle Ludwig brought me to the Christmas Eve party. I was but a boy, but I remember her clearly. And I was thrilled when she returned with him."

"I would have kept in touch, Klaus, but you didn't exactly give me an address that night." She giggled, playing it up for her parents' sake.

"What can I say? I was young and foolish." They tore their eyes away from one another and looked at her parents.

"Papa?" Clara licked her suddenly dry lips.

Her father hesitated. "Is this more amenable to you than — than the other arrangement we discussed?"

He was really considering it? A weight lifted off her chest as she nodded her head furiously. "I know it seems fast, but Papa, I love him."

Godfather Drosselmeyer smiled warmly at them, then at her father. "The fates work in mysterious ways."

Papa nodded. "You have my blessing, Your Highness." Mama turned to him as the color drained from her face, and he patted her arm. "I need to speak with Baron von Galen, my love. I'll return shortly." She merely nodded as he strode away.

"We don't need to advertise Klaus's title. His kingdom is quite small, and I guarantee no one's heard of it." Hopefully Godfather Drosselmeyer hadn't broken any rules telling Papa and Mama that Klaus was a prince.

"But it's such an honor." Goodness, Mama was laying it on thick.

"It's fine, Mrs. Stahlbaum. Süssland is, as Clara said, small."

"And I'd want to marry him whether he was a prince or not." Clara rushed her words out.

Mama frowned at that. Too bad. "I see. Well, why don't you go on and enjoy the party? We can make arrangements to pack up your things."

The band struck up a waltz, and Klaus drew her further into the room. "Happy New Year to you, Mrs. Stahlbaum."

"A Happy New Year to you as well, Klaus. Be sure you treat my daughter well."

"Of course." He turned to her. "May I have this dance, darling?"

"You can have all my dances, my love."

As they swept over the dance floor, she gazed up at her husband. "Are you sure you want another wedding, Klaus? Most men wouldn't want to put up with the fuss."

"My dearest Clara, I am not a man. And if it makes things easier with your family, of course, we'll have another wedding."

"Few women get to marry their husband twice," she snickered.

Out of the corner of her eye, she spotted Baron von Galen and Papa in conversation. The Baron called Berengar over, and then Klaus spun her around.

"Don't pay attention to that swine, darling. He's nothing now."

"You realize the only reason my parents agreed is because of your title?"

Klaus shrugged. "It might as well be useful. Even if no one else knows." He pressed her tighter into his chest. "What would you have done if they'd said no?"

"Run away with you anyway and apologized for eloping." She giggled at the thought of her Mama getting a note that her quiet, bookish daughter had done something so rebellious. "At least we won't have to pretend for long."

"Yes, I'll need to discuss the ruse with my parents. I assume they're expected as well?"

"Of course… oh dear. Godfather Drosselmeyer will need to make a lot of those pocket watches."

Klaus only smiled at her. "I doubt he'll mind."

Adelia and Francesca arrived at the last minute, finding her in Klaus's arms. Her friends latched onto her hands and dragged her off the dance floor. "Excuse us, sir." He just chuckled and followed behind them at a stroll. They pulled her into a huddle next to one of the stone pillars.

"Clara! Who is *that*?" Francesca whispered furiously.

She suppressed a giggle. "Can you both keep a secret?"

"Of course!" Adelia looked back over her shoulder at Klaus, who was now in conversation with their husbands.

Clara leaned close and whispered to her friends. "That's my husband."

Squeals erupted, but Clara hushed them quickly. "Mama and Papa don't know we're already wed."

"Clara, how scandalous!"

"To think you, of all people, would *elope*!"

She placed a finger to her lips. "Not a word out of either of you. We're having a proper wedding, but you can't tell anyone."

"You look so happy, my friend."

"You're positively glowing!"

"So then, the rumors were false?"

Clara looked between her two dear friends. "What rumors?"

Adelia bit her lip. She and Francesca glanced at each other, then at Clara. "The servants were saying something about you being engaged to Berengar. We thought perhaps you'd run away."

"And we wouldn't blame you for a minute." Francesca shuddered.

"Heidi!" Clara palmed her face. "Heavens, she shouldn't have said anything."

"Wait. It's true?"

She gave her friends a small shrug. "Not anymore."

They both breathed a sigh of relief.

"Well, you certainly found a handsome replacement."

"Indeed, I did." Then she remembered the letters she'd written to her friends. They were unnecessary now. "Klaus is from Godfather Drosselmeyer's country, and we have to return tonight. I won't be able to come visit except for Christmas. And there's no post out there." Adelia blinked back tears.

Francesca was a bit more pragmatic. "Are you taking Heidi with you?"

"I can't. She can't follow me that far." Clara looked into her friends' faces. "If she'll go, can one of you please hire Heidi away from here? She's not exactly Mother's favorite."

Francesca nodded, a sneaky smile spreading across her face. "I'll speak to the housekeeper and see what we can do. If she's good with children, I'm going to need a nanny soon." Clara grinned as Adelia squealed at the news. Then she led her friends back to their men so she could introduce Klaus to her friends properly, before her husband stole her back to the dance floor.

That night was the best party Clara had ever attended at her parents' home. It had to be partly thanks to her husband's presence, but also because of her newfound confidence. Her mother remarked once or twice at the change in her daughter, which Clara ignored.

Heidi would pack all of her dresses and jewelry in a trunk, which Clara promised to send a carriage for as soon as possible. Her mother didn't seem to question her duty to this new queen, for which Clara was thankful.

At a few minutes to midnight came the announcement she'd once dreaded.

His unsuspecting father-in-law called for a toast just before the clock struck twelve. One week ago, Klaus had anxiously awaited that chime, so that he could take his flesh and blood form instead of his wooden Nutcracker. He kept one possessive arm around Clara's waist as her Papa raised a glass.

"Good evening everyone. As the year changes, so do we. It is my pleasure to announce my daughter Clara's engagement to the honorable Klaus von Süssland! Welcome to the family." Applause broke out among the revelers. Klaus took his cues from Clara, and when she curtsied, he gave a small bow.

When the hour struck and the old grandfather clock sounded twelve, everyone shouted, "Happy New Year!"

Many women known to the family approached Clara to congratulate her on her engagement. They went with the explanation that they had given her parents, omitting his title. Trying to explain where the Land of Sweets and Toys was would ruin the secrecy that kept his homeland safe. It was easy to explain he was Drosselmeyer's great-nephew and that he'd become enamored with her during their travels.

It wasn't that far from the truth, after all.

As the hour grew later, and Clara yawned, he hooked her arm through his. "Darling, you wanted to show me the gardens, didn't you?"

"Of course." They strolled to the back of the room, where a set of French doors let them out onto a small patio. "They're not very interesting in winter, of course."

"I just wanted to get you alone for a few minutes."

She giggled. "I need to try something."

"What's that?"

She walked backwards to the edge of the patio, closed her eyes, and then pushed her hand behind her back. With that, beautiful multi-colored magic shot up from her hand and burst into the sky.

"Clara! How did you..."

"You know how, Klaus." She grinned at her achievement. "It's traditional to set off fireworks for the New Year, but Papa was always worried about the danger."

"My clever wife." Klaus joined her at the edge of the terrace. "You're going to freeze out here. Let's go back inside."

"First, look up."

He did as she asked. A sprig of mistletoe had escaped the after-Christmas cleaning. "Well, we can't ignore that." Klaus drew her into his arms and held her close. "I'll just have to keep you warm."

Then he slanted his mouth over hers, and her giggles turned to a hum of pleasure. Regretfully, he kept the kiss short for propriety's sake. They would have all the time in the world once they arrived back home.

Epilogue

The Sugar Plum Palace was a whirl of activity, and Clara hated to leave them.

"Are you excited about tomorrow?"

Galiena had decided it was time to step down. Klaus had explained that since the land had accepted Clara, it was best for her to abdicate. She would still be around in an advisory capacity, which made her only slightly less nervous.

She bit her lip. "Of course."

Galiena patted her shoulder. "It's alright to be nervous. I was shaking in my shoes when my mother abdicated. And I grew up here with the expectation of ruling one day." That was a very different situation from Clara's.

It had been a year packed full of training with Mother Gingerbread and the Sugar Plum Fairy, and now Galiena had declared her ready to rule her adopted homeland.

The coronation was to take place on Christmas Day, but Clara and Klaus had promised to attend the Stahlbaum Christmas Eve party with Godfather Ludwig.

"Are you sure it's alright for us to leave, Galiena?"

The reigning Sugar Plum Fairy waved her off. "Everything is well in hand. Besides, you have to tell your parents the good news!"

Her heart fluttered in her chest just thinking about it. She hadn't seen her parents since her second wedding.

Klaus knocked on the door to his mother's study. "Darling, we should get ready. Uncle Ludwig will meet us at the carriage in an hour."

"I'm coming!" She quickly hugged her mother-in-law. "We'll be back tonight."

"Have a great time, and give your parents my regards."

"I will!"

Her husband strode alongside her as she hurried to their suite. "Trixie is waiting for us."

"I can only imagine what she's cooked up for me to wear." Her favorite blue pixie had finished her Tinkerer training, focusing on clothing, and she loved to create fantastic gowns with her magic for her Sugar Plum Princess. Trixie had a flair for the dramatic, which was fine for the Realm of Dreams, but in the Realm of Waking Clara didn't dare wear anything outlandish.

They met Rose coming down the stairs, chasing her little one. "Mama isn't done yet!"

Clara grabbed onto the pup, and he squealed as she lifted him into the air. "Did you interrupt Mama's cleaning again?" Rose was working as a maid part-time, and apprenticing under Cook the rest of the time.

"I'm sorry, Princess."

"Don't worry about it. How's training?"

"I'm almost certified!" she squeaked with pride. Galiena and Farolf's exchange program had been a tremendous success, and the thought of continuing it thrilled Clara.

"That's great! You have a lovely night. We have to go home for my parents' party."

Rose waved at them and continued to admonish her son in their native tongue before carrying him back to where she had been hard at work.

Klaus ushered her into their apartment, where Trixie hovered in wait. "There you are! Just wait till you see what I did with the red gown!" Clara followed her, careful to avoid the pixie dust from her wings.

On the bed lay her crimson silk gown, the bertha now enhanced with tiny ruby jewels along the edge of the lace. She'd fashioned a broach of holly at the center, and tiny holly embroidery along the hem of the skirt.

"Trixie, this is gorgeous! It's perfect!"

The pixie grinned. "I thought you'd like it."

"You're not allowed to change it now, I hope you realize."

She somersaulted in mid-air, then landed on the ground and pulled her wings in. "Let's get you changed."

Klaus was more than happy to help Trixie remove her day dress. They added a couple of petticoats and slid the precious gown over her head. Then he dressed himself in his matching military style coat while Trixie used her magic on Clara's hair.

Once their outerwear was in place, Klaus and Clara met Godfather Ludwig in the courtyard. The staff hitched two mares from the royal stables to a white carriage. Her godfather held the reins while a stable hand opened the door for them.

"On to the Stahlbaum house!"

Clara snuggled next to Klaus in the cozy carriage. While her parents knew Klaus was a prince, they still didn't know where his country lay. Although they had tried to insist on visiting.

Drosselmeyer had to sit down and spin quite the yarn for Friedrich and Margareta Stahlbaum that danced around the truth. Whether they would accept it, time would only tell. But their daughter showed up in good health and fine clothes, and that seemed to assuage Papa's worries.

Especially now that Mama's attention was on her little brother. Apparently, he'd gotten drunk a few too many times at the local tavern and embarrassed her.

It couldn't happen to someone more deserving.

They pulled up in front of her parents' manor house, and Clara took Klaus's hand to step down from the carriage. He had grown somewhat possessive since the Healers made their discovery, and she had to admit it gave her a thrill. She knew he trusted her strength, but the fact he *wanted* to take care of her meant everything.

Godfather Drosselmeyer let them go ahead as he hefted his sack of presents for the children from the seat. Inside, Mama had decorated to the nines as always, holly hanging in every corner and the evergreen boughs over the doors. Servants she didn't recognize took their coats, and she and Klaus met her parents in the drawing room.

"Merry Christmas, Mama, Papa... Fritz." Fritz stood at Papa's side, a dour expression on his face. Without her to play hostess with Mama, it was apparently his duty now.

"Merry Christmas, my dear." Papa and Mama embraced her, her brother only offering a nod.

"We have some good news for you," Klaus prompted her.

Clara couldn't contain her joy. "You're going to be grandparents!"

Her mother kissed her on both cheeks and Papa shook Klaus's hand, then embraced him like a son. After they completed their congratulations, Klaus whisked her away to the party. They watched Godfather Ludwig passing out his beloved toys that he worked on all year, and danced to the music the band played.

In the carriage on the way home, Klaus tucked her under his arm and nibbled on her neck. "Are you ready to become everyone's queen, not just mine?"

She laughed as his lips tickled her. "I don't know that I'll ever be ready."

"You're going to be amazing." His kisses traveled up her neck to that spot behind her ear that made her melt.

"Klaus, can't you wait till we get home?"

"I've waited all night, wife." He took her mouth next, his tongue licking inside. She pushed him away with great difficulty, and then he pouted.

"It hardly takes any time to get home, husband," she chided him.

"Very well, my love. But you're mine as soon as we get back to our suite."

"I'm always yours, Klaus." She shivered as he ran a hand over the back of her neck, then smiled as he pressed the back of her hand to his lips.

"As I am yours, my darling."

Lost in her Nutcracker's eyes, Clara didn't even notice Godfather Drosselmeyer driving the carriage through the portal back to the Realm of Dreams, and the Land of Sweets and Toys.

Klaus hopped out as soon as they stopped in front of the palace and held out his hand. Time to take his wife back to their suite and show her what that ruby red gown did to him.

"Good night, Uncle!" He waved to Ludwig, who passed the reins to the stable hand that greeted them. Then he hurried into the palace proper, up the stairs to their apartment.

Sometimes he wondered if he'd wake up from this amazing dream and find that the Mouse King's darkness still reigned over the realm. Yet every morning he awoke to find his Clara in his bed, and he thanked the Goddess for this life.

His incredibly alluring wife who was pregnant with his child.

Locking the suite's doors behind them, he threw her cloak to the floor and pressed kisses to her neck. Her shiver told him she was as aroused as he, and he started making quick work of the hooks at the back of her dress.

"Klaus, darling… the bedroom is *right there*."

"Can't wait," he murmured as the last hook slid open and he dropped her bodice to lick and kiss the swells of her breasts. He lifted the red gown and laid it on a nearby chair, then hefted her petticoats above her head.

"Don't you dare rip those laces! Trixie will yell at you tomorrow morning."

Klaus growled in her ear as he loosened the corset, then it too came off, and he finally had access to his wife. She might feign a protest, but she loved it when he pressed her against the wall and tore her drawers off, then kneeled at her feet and licked the entrance to heaven.

Her nails dug into his scalp as she moaned. She'd been even more enticing since her pregnancy. Something about knowing she carried his baby made her all the easier to arouse, and he sucked the evidence off her lower lips until her walls pulsed around his finger. "Klaus, I'm going to — Ahh!" With one more suck of her tiny nub, she shook above him, and he gently lowered her leg off his shoulder to let her stand on her own. Rising, he shed his own clothes quickly while his beautiful bride basked in her afterglow. Then he picked her up and carried her over to the bedroom, his member bouncing in the air.

Klaus laid her on their bed and stroked her hair. She hummed. "You're not done yet, husband." Then Clara pulled him over her body and he sank gratefully between her thighs, thrusting gently into her heat. Nails in his ass spurred him to take her faster, harder, until they both cried out as he erupted into her, coating her womb with his seed again.

He took the pins out of his wife's golden hair, and the two sated lovebirds curled up under the blankets. "Happy Christmas, my love."

"Happy Christmas, my Nutcracker Prince."

Thank you for reading Clara and Klaus's story! I'd be honored if you'd leave a review.

Notes from Jasmine

This book was two years in the making. It started when I read Aidy Award's *Protected*, a Nutcracker retelling. She's one of my favorite authors and such an inspiration. Then, my husband and I went down to the basement to watch a filmed version of the Nutcracker ballet. And I found myself asking, "what if the prince went back for Clara? What would drive him to do so?"

I ran upstairs as the credits rolled, and I was typing until one in the morning.

There's not much to say about this one. I hope it brought you some holiday spirit and reminded you of the wonder of the season.

Many thanks to N. A. Hyde and Patty Web for their critiques. Fantasy authors are a different species altogether, and I'm so grateful for you.

Much love for my beta team, who read this when the weather was definitely not conducive to a holiday romance. You guys rock.

Thanks again to Jenn, my amazing editor, who worked two books into her schedule simultaneously so I could achieve my goal of releasing this book on my dad's birthday.

Shout out to my friends on the Self Publishing with Dale L. Roberts Discord server, and my Romance Writer's Club server.

And last, but definitely never least, all my love to my husband for his unending support.

I hope you all have a magical holiday season.

XOXO,

Jasmine

About the Author

Jasmine is a lover of all things romance. Normally, she writes contemporary romance but is an equal-opportunity reader of most romance genres. When she's not reading or writing, you can find her baking or playing board games with her friends and family. She lives in Pennsylvania with her patient husband and too many books. Find her online at www.jasmineccaldwell.com

Also By Jasmine

For a current list of my available titles, scan the QR code below:

www.ingramcontent.com/pod-product-compliance
Lightning Source LLC
Chambersburg PA
CBHW032027310726

48972CB00002B/569